Wildlife Warriors
United !

xoxo —
E.G. Yenin

RAYNE'S

(WILD!) LIFE ADVENTURES

A Wildlife Warrior Series
Book One

E.G. YERIAN

ISBN: 978-1-66784-151-9 (paperback)

ISBN: 978-1-66784-152-6 (eBook)

CONTENTS

1: Destiny Strikes

Do you believe in fate? I do, and I'll tell you why. When I was 8 years old I was almost fatally struck by a ferociously power- ful lightning bolt as I was running to my house seeking shelter from an approaching storm. It hit me from behind, striking the ground directly beneath my feet with such great force I went flying high into the air before face-planting on to the wet grass while simultaneously sliding through it like I was on an electrically charged slip & slide. It's a good thing I was running fast and didn't get directly hit by the lightning because if so I would clearly not still be here on Planet Earth to tell you all about it. At least that's what I overheard the Doctor say to my Mom when they thought I was sleeping. You can hear a lot from adults when you pretend you're not listening, but in that instance I think I could have lived without knowing that little nugget of information. The Doctor said it was quite the miracle I survived the lightning strike suffering a concussion, broken arm, and second-degree burns on the back of my legs. I also had the most pain- ful, gnarly looking wet grass road rash on the entire front of my body. As remarkable as all that is, it pales in comparison to the profound experience I had that day while I was lying face down in the grass unconscious, out like a light. While in the darkness of unconsciousness my life literally flashed before my eyes. I still find it hard to describe but it was like I was wearing a virtual reality headset while watching a video movie of my life~my past, my present, AND my future.

To this day even though I can't remember details of the visions, I know innately that in the case of my life, everything happens for a reason and makes perfect sense. Days later after the accident I told my mom about my experience. She called it my destiny, and said we are all masters of our own destiny. I thought that was very fitting and believed it to be true. Still to this day my 15 year old self takes some comfort in knowing this even when life brings me the worst tragedy. When I woke up later in the hospital my mom told me the first thing I said to her was, "Mom I'm going to get married in the future!!! I don't want to get married!" before bawling my eyes out. She told me it took everything in her not to laugh because I was so dramatic about it. She expected me to be crying from my injuries, not from the knowledge of my very distant nuptials. To be completely honest it still freaks me out. I may eventually get married but I'm going to make darn sure it's a long time in the future. I have a lot of living to do before I settle down, lots of adventures to go on. I know this because I saw it.

After my unfortunate encounter with a super charged fire-bolt my mom told me she started noticing new things about my personality that really surprised and delighted her. Before that shocking event happened I always wanted to stay inside, voraciously reading endless amounts of books and sometimes playing video games. I was very introverted and borderline shy, refusing to play with other kids in the neighborhood. (Case in point, when the lightning struck me I was running from my neighbors house to my home because I was bored playing barbies with the girl next door.) After coming home from the hospital she said she couldn't keep me from going outside to explore our neighborhood environment, spending hours upon hours among the plants, trees and animals. Nature became fascinating to me, I could see more clearly the vibrant beauty of the leaves on the branches of trees, their shapes, their colors. I know this is crazy strange but it was almost as if I could see them pulsing from the energy of the sun. I started studying bees, watching them pollinate the flowers, then take the nectar to the hives high up in the trees. The bees needed the flowers for food, the flowers needed the bees to reproduce. I asked my mom to buy me a book about bees so that I could understand them better. Turns out they're fascinating! If I saw a snake in my backyard, I wasn't afraid in the slightest but so curious to know more about it like, where did it live? What does it eat, why does it stretch out in the sun? (because it's cold blooded and they need the heat.) Just like a snake when it was warm outside I could lie in the grass for hours. Occasionally an animal would come near me as if to say "Hi, I see you!" before slowly scampering away. I especially liked the visits from raccoons, they are such clever little scoundrels! I could watch their shenanigans all day long and never get bored. I never attempted to touch any wildlife out of respect, always observing from a distance. I never interfered unless absolutely necessary, like the time I kept hearing distress calls from what sounded like a baby bird from the trees behind my house. I followed those cries until I spotted it on the ground at the base of a very tall tree. It was just a tiny fuzzball of a baby bird, it didn't even have all of its feathers yet. A baby bird is quite amusing to look at, it will almost make you laugh out loud it's so funny looking. I was astonished it fell so far down and was still alive, but it was and I had to rescue it. Here's the thing, I don't know how but I knew what I had to do. I ran home to the shed behind my house to grab a small basket and a long ladder to climb the tree to the nest. I have to tell you it was quite the struggle, the aluminum ladder was heavy and twice my size but somehow I managed to drag it to the tree where the baby bird was. The nest was really high up in the tree branches, I knew what I was about to do was dangerous and that my mom would be so mad at me if she knew what I was about to do. I did not care. I was intently focused on saving the baby bird and reuniting it with its mother. I placed the very heavy ladder against the tree as sturdy as I could get it, then very gently picked up the baby bird to place it in the basket I brought. I climbed up that ladder against the tree with one hand and two very shaky legs. I sighed a huge sigh of relief when I successfully reached the nest to place the baby bird back in it. I had heard before that you should never touch a baby bird or that a mother will abandon it, but again I instinctively knew that wasn't true. I was right, when I placed the baby back with its mom the reunion was joyous, I could tell by their chatter and chirping. She also started feeding it. It was a beautiful moment.

The ordeal of the somewhat dangerous rescue was worth the fierce scolding I got from my mother when she saw me dragging the heavy ladder back to the house. She told me she was disappointed that I didn't come and get her, but she was proud that I was brave enough to do something so wonderful. I didn't regret doing it and knew I would do it again in a heartbeat. There were many more small successful wildlife rescues I would make in the next seven years before the worst day of my life happened. The idyllic childhood I lived would soon be shattered by the most devastating news one could ever receive.

2: The Ritz

"Rayne Lanecastor please report to the front desk!" The voice on the intercom system in my math class blared. My heart skipped a beat because I was extremely worried about my mom who was battling Breast Cancer for the second time, she was very sick. Here's the thing about cancer, it's relentlessly scary and it wrecks people's lives. My mom always tried to hide her pain from me, but I could see it on her face sometimes when she thought I wasn't looking. I pray every day that someone, somehow, can find a cure for this terrible disease. As I approached the office I instantly relaxed when I saw my mom's short strawberry blonde hair. She lost her hair when she endured Chemo but it was growing back. She looked a little tired, but she glowed with excitement.

"Hi Mom, what are you doing here?"

"I'm here to kidnap you so we can spend the day together!"

"Awesome! What a nice surprise!" I replied, thrilled to be sprung from my high school on a Friday unexpectedly, especially from algebra class. I freaking hate math class.

"I also brought you a present, I can't wait to give it to you!" She looked happy. That made me happy.

"So what are we doing, mom?" I was curious to know.

"I've booked a suite at the Ritz Carlton Resort. We are going to pamper ourselves at the spa and order room service – – – quality mom and daughter time!"

"Wow! Fun! It's been some time since we have done that. I love the Ritz!"

"I love it too and you know my motto...work hard, reward yourself!"

Twenty minutes later she pulled into the Ritz. A courteous Valet greeted us at the entrance.

"Welcome to the Ritz Carlton, please enjoy your stay."

"We will, thank you." My mom said to him handing him the car keys.

"I packed your pj's and toothbrush and booked us mani's and pedi's! This is going to be so fun! We deserve it."

We checked in and went to our Suite, which was both luxurious and comfortable. I immediately jumped on the fluffy bed.

"This room is sooooo nice mom thanks for doing this!"

"Honey there is nothing I wouldn't do for you, I love you. It has been too long since we've done this, way too long."

I knew what she was thinking but not saying, not since she was diagnosed with the dreaded "C" word, Cancer.

A couple hours later after getting the full pampered treatment at the Ritz Spa we went back to our suite, changed into our pajama's and ordered room service. We ordered Wild Alaska Salmon with a lemon dill sauce and asparagus which was delicious, then we finished our meal with 3 different desserts; creme brûlée, white chocolate raspberry cheesecake, and a chocolate mousse so decadently delicious I licked the parfait dish it was in after I had devoured it! When we could eat no more we settled on the king size bed with the fluffy Duvet and oversized pillows. That's when my mom handed me my present. It was wrapped in glittery silver paper and was rectangular in shape.

"What is this, mom?"

"Open it up Rayne, then I'll explain why I got it for you."

I ripped the paper apart quickly, exposing a white cardboard box with the silver Apple Logo on one side and the word iPad on the other.

"An iPad! Mom I love it!" I opened the box to look at the sleek white tablet my mom bought for me.

"Look on the back, Rayne, there is something I want you to see."

I turned the iPad over, noticing some engraved words at the top. I read aloud the message:

To my beloved daughter Rayne, Love Always and Forever, Mom.

I felt tears forming in my eyes, the words were beautiful and meant so much to me.

"Thank you mom, I love you always and forever too." I managed to mumble.

"I bought it for you Rayne for many reasons. It's time for us to have a serious conversation about the future, which is bright for you but limited for me. I have been planning this for quite some time because I feel you are mature enough and certainly smart enough at age 15 to understand now."

She then said the words I did not want to hear.

"I am going to die, Rayne, and soon. I've tried my best to fight the Cancer but it has spread. I need to prepare you for what lies ahead. Please, sweetie, do not cry after I'm gone because the last thing I ever want for you is unhappiness. Every time you start to feel sad please think of me and know that I can only be happy in Heaven knowing you're happy. Please promise me you will be!" She fervently exclaimed.

"I promise, mom, I promise!" I broke down, crying my heart out. I didn't want to, but the emotions were too powerful to be denied. My mom held me the entire time, stroking my hair with soothing motions. She didn't cry, she stayed strong for me. When I could cry no more she turned on the iPad to show me what she had set up on it already, she had been working on writing me letters in the "Notes" app on the tablet.

"See this, Rayne?" She opened the note app and started reading the first note she wrote to me.

"What True Love Is"

True Love is a rare and wondrous experience! I had it with your father, the love of my life. You never knew him, as you know he died in a car accident when you were just a baby, but he was a magnificent man, both passionate and compassionate! When he passed I knew without a shadow of a doubt that I would never love another man the way I loved him. Our love lasted a decade, and we had you. Losing him taught me that life was not fair, and that it can be so emotionally painful, painful to the point of despair. I also discovered that emotional pain hurts a hundred times more than physical pain~deep despair will kill you coldly if you let it! (Don't you ever let it, Rayne!) I wasn't going to let it get the better of me because I had you. Every time I thought it might, all I had to do was look at you to see how much you looked like him; you have the very same small dimple to the left of your lips, the same deeply intense emerald green eyes flecked with little dots of gold. You both were gifted with the incredibly attractive ability to show your feelings clearly through the expressions of your eyes! Whenever I looked at you after he passed I would immediately feel the overwhelming and welcoming strength I needed to carry on. Rayne, you were my salvation. I was so grateful for two things, my timeless love with your father, and my unconditional love for you.

True Love is one of the very best experiences about life, an experience that will enhance your every emotion! It can actually make you feel like every nerve in your body is tingling from your head to your toes. Sometimes true love happens in an instant, you know you love that person as soon as you lay your eyes upon them. Sometimes true love grows at a snails pace, tried and true. How will you recognize it, you may wonder? I can only tell you how I did. I was lucky enough to experience it twice, once with my "First Love" when I was 21, and then again when I met your dad. My first true love relationship lasted a couple of years, unfortunately we were just too young and immature about life to make it work. I loved him deeply, from the first moment I saw him. Our eyes connected and that was it. The phrase "love at first sight" is very true. We had chemistry and passion, he loved me deeply as well. I knew without asking that he loved me and I him. Please always wait and take your time before giving any part of yourself, especially your kisses. Do not even consider falling in love until you are 100% sure the person you are with is absolutely and completely in love with you, and you feel the same. Otherwise it is just meaningless. You are special. True love is worth waiting for. The ultimate breakup with my first love was very painful. There might be a time one day Rayne when you feel heartbreak, I won't lie-it is just about the worst feeling ever. Most people do not get a pass from heartbreak, it's just a part of life. I can laugh now, but when I experienced it I spent days crying like a fool! I also lost 10 pounds because I couldn't eat for weeks after the breakup. Eventually the hurt passed leaving me grateful for having shared that love, the good, the great, AND the bad. Six years after that I met your dad, Ray Lanecastor, my eternal soul mate. This time I knew it was forever. We got married and the 10 years with him were the absolute best years of my life. We created you, the most wonderful gift I ever received. Rayne, your father loved you with all his heart and soul, he was the best father a man could ever be, a man of very high moral character. He was the complete package. I loved him with every fiber of my body, still do. I want the same for you, Rayne, I want you to know what true love is. I know you will find it because you are a beautiful person inside and out. Wait on it, take your time finding it, and sometimes, it just finds you.

My mom finished reading the note then showed me all the other "Notes" she had written for me. There were quite a few, she told me she had written them for the past few weeks whenever she thought of something she wanted me to know about life. She asked me to look at them in the future using what I could as guidance, to read any of them to cheer me up when I felt sad, or when I needed reassurance of her eternal love and support.

During that conversation she broached the subject of where I was going to live after she passed. She told me who my new guardians would be, my Uncle Bart and Aunt Beth who live in Florida, her home state. My mom and dad moved to Ohio when he was offered a job as a Marine Biologist working at the Cleveland Zoo. I was born soon after.

"I met your dad when he worked for your Uncle Bart, we fell in love and got married. When your father was offered his dream job in Cleveland we moved. It was hard at first for me to adjust to Ohio winters, I was born and raised in Florida after all!" She laughed, then continued.

"You know I always keep in close contact with my sister Beth. We were inseparable as children-you two are the most important people in my life! You also know how lovely your Aunt Beth is, she loves you very much. I asked her to be your guardian, she said she wouldn't have it any other way and was deeply honored to be given such a gift. It gives me peace of mind, Rayne, to know you will be so loved and well taken care of."

"I'm going to live in Florida, mom?" I'm not going to lie, I was starting to freak out a little bit.

"Think of it as a grand new adventure Rayne, as you know they live on property of a Florida Wildlife Park where Bart is the Park Manager and Beth is the Education Director. We have visited Florida several times-it's one of your favorite places to take vacation. You will make new friends-three teenagers around your age are living on property too, the Assistant Manager and Wildlife Supervisor's kids."

Watching my mother get so animated with excitement started to make me curious, but it was so much to absorb I felt stunned.

"There's more, they have a Junior Wildlife Ranger Academy program now for kids age 14 thru 17. Think about how much you love animals! Now you will get to learn how to work with them."

That *was* intriguing, I thought. "They don't mind me living with them?"

"Mind? Rayne, they insist. You are family, they love you. They emailed me pictures of your new room-you are going to love it, I'm not exaggerating. The house they live in was built in the 1960's, it has 3 stories, the top floor is all your space! It has wood floors, brick walls, exposed beams on the ceiling, even a small kitchen and bathroom! The top floor was converted into an efficiency type of apartment for students interning at the Wildlife Park, but now they stay at the new Wildlife Care building that was recently built. It's charming, spacious, and all yours. I will show you the pictures when we get home."

She could see I was trying hard to digest all of this information so she said one last thing to me that I will never forget.

"I'm sorry, Rayne, that I am leaving you soon. You are the most amazing daughter a mother could ever ask for, I'm so proud of the strong young woman that you have become. I need you to understand that knowing you are about to go live with our family in Florida gives me such joy, such comfort. You are about to embark on an incredible adventure- please enjoy and appreciate every minute of it! I Love you forever my sweet Rayne."

She pulled me into a hug holding me close to her when she was finished talking. I told her I loved her too. She lightened up the mood by making me a japanese cherry blossom scented bubble bath (my favorite!) in the huge jetted tub so that I could have some quiet private time to process our talk. When I finished soaking in the tub I felt relaxed yet resigned to face the inevitable sorrow ahead. She rented a romantic comedy to watch on the HD flat screen T.V. then we stayed up all night talking about anything and everything before I fell into a deep sleep. It was the most profound and wonderful night that I will never forget.

3: A Last Goodbye

"Rayne? Are you alright?" My Aunt Beth lightly tapped on the bathroom stall door. I was definitely *not* alright, because my mother was dying, but I wouldn't let my aunt know that because she was undoubtedly dealing with her own deep sorrow right now.

"I'm fine Aunt Beth, I'll be out in just a few minutes I promise." I tried my best to not answer her with a shaky voice. I could hear her deep sigh of relief when I answered her.

"The Hospital Chaplain is here to visit and pray for your mom. I think it would be good for you to meet him, so come out when you're ready honey." She spoke softly to me on the other side of the door, then left the bathroom.

I grabbed more toilet paper to dry my tears and blow my already sore nose. I'd spent the last 20 minutes in this refuge of a bathroom stall crying, praying, and trying not to be overcome with grief and despair. I never felt more helpless. Why is this happening again to me? Is it not enough that I already lost my father when I was just a baby, never getting a chance to know him? I knew without a shadow of a doubt that my mom was going to die now too and there wasn't anything I could do to prevent it. Knowing that made me bend over again with wracking, silent sobs that left me gasping for air. Breathe Rayne, Breathe! *DO NOT BREAK DOWN AGAIN!* I gained control of my traitorous emotions once more but it wasn't easy, it took every bit of strength I could muster. I couldn't believe this was happening, but it definitely was. I regretfully left the bathroom stall that had given me private harbor to let it all go while hiding it. I headed over to one of the bathroom sinks and turned on the cold water to splash on my face, hoping it would help erase all traces of my seemingly endless tears. As I patted my face dry with the scratchy brown paper towel pulled from the dispenser, I took a good look at my face in the mirror. What stared back at me I didn't recognize. My skin was death-like pale, highlighted with bright red splotches, especially around my eyes where I had continually wiped them. The purple-black circles under my swollen eyes reminded me of a Panda Bear minus the cuteness. On top of that, my expression was of the worst kind-one of deep pain and sorrow. How appropriate, I thought, to look so awful when facing doom and despair. It was time to say goodbye to my mom, delaying would not stop the inevitable. *Help me God, Please! I beg you!* I fervently prayed yet again. I took a few more deep breaths to gain my composure as much as possible. With leaded feet I headed back to my moms hospital room.

The moment I met the hospital Chaplain I felt at ease. I sensed that he was a good man, his kind eyes and sympathetic demeanor showed he cared deeply about my sorrow. The compassion emanating from him helped to calm my horribly painful emotions and I stopped crying for the moment. He gently explained that he was there to pray for my mother, and for me as well. He asked me if I had any questions, I told him I did.

"I don't know how to say goodbye, how can I possibly do that? I don't want to!" I cried out. "Everyone keeps saying 'You're being so strong, Rayne' but I'm not! I'm NOT strong and I don't want to be! I don't have the strength to do this, I can't!" I looked at my mother who I loved so dearly laying there so still, barely breathing. She was dying, and on a morphine drip to ease her transition to death. "Do you think she can even hear me?"

"I don't know for sure Rayne, but I strongly believe it is possible. Why don't I pray for you, to help ease your pain and give you strength. Would you like that?" He looked my way. I nodded yes.

"Dear Heavenly Father..." he prayed, his words becoming a soothing balm to my soul. A welcoming comfort took over me, but again my tears fell uncontrollably down my face. We held hands, the Chaplain, my mother and I. When he finished his beautiful prayer I saw a single tear run down my mothers cheek, even though her eyes were closed and she seemed to not be aware of her surroundings. I gently brushed her tear away, told her I loved her forever, and kissed her one last time. A short hour later my heart shattered into a million pieces when she died, leaving me desolate and alone. I was now quite possibly one of the most pathetically sad orphans to ever exist. I had no clue what would happen from this point on, but I promised my mom to get past this sadness and embrace what would come next, so that is exactly what I was going to do. I walked out of the hospital and never looked back.

4: Florida Bound

The drive from my hometown of Cleveland, Ohio to my future home at Homosassa, Florida gave me plenty of time to think about my future. I was at a loss trying to imagine what my future consisted of but thankfully the two passengers in the front seats of the black Toyota Prius we were driving in were trying their very best to give me some idea.

"How much do you know about my job in Florida, Rayne?" The driver of the Prius, my Uncle Bart, asked. His warm blue eyes briefly met mine via the rear view mirror before turning his attention back to the open road before us.

"I know you are the Manager of a Florida Wildlife Park called the Homosassa Springs State Wildlife Park and that you, Aunt Beth, and Aiden live there." Aiden is their son, my 12 year old cousin. He is a super sweet kid with light brown wavy hair and eyes the same color as his dad. I can't believe I am going to live with him and his mom and dad, but I am.

"That's right Rayne, it's your home now too. I hope you will love it."

"She will love it Bart, just like we do!" My aunt added looking at me. "It's a magical, beautiful paradise, Rayne, I can't wait to show it to you." Her infectious enthusiasm made me crack a smile for the first time in weeks, but just for a brief second.

"I know I will love it, Aunt Beth, I'm so very grateful. My mom wanted me to look at it as my very first exciting life adventure, so she gave me this iPad to record my new life in Florida." I showed them my treasured iPad given to me by my mother before she died. "She thought it would be a great tool to help look up the environment and wildlife that live in Florida. I love it."

What I didn't tell them was that my mom also left me the letters of wisdom and love on my iPad, because that was something I wanted to keep private. Just thinking about my mom made my heart hurt again. I wondered if that sadness would ever go away. I honestly didn't think so. As we cruised down the charcoal grey highway we came across a billboard stating "Welcome to the Sunshine State" greeting us as warmly as the midday sun. It was getting so warm I shed the Nike hoodie I was wearing. My Aunt Beth said we were getting closer to my new home. Looking at Google maps on my iPad showed me that we would be heading southwest, along the Gulf of Mexico side of Florida. The other side of Florida heading east is surrounded by the Atlantic Ocean, and Orlando, (my mother affectionately called it "Mickey Mouse town") is centrally located sandwiched in between the two great bodies of waters. Our destination was Homosassa Springs, a small rural town situated around the Homosassa River, a river connected to the Gulf of Mexico, known for its fresh water springs and home to huge Manatee populations. I took this time to look up more facts about Florida. I already knew it was home to alligators, manatee's, orange groves, pristine sandy beaches, and many entertainment theme parks, but I was curious to read what else the internet could teach me about Florida so I went to google on my iPad to research it. According to the internet, Florida (nicknamed the Sunshine State) has a population of approximately 20 million citizens and is the fourth most populous state in America. Florida has the longest coastline in the United States, it is the only state that borders both the Gulf of Mexico and the Atlantic Ocean. Much of the state is at or near sea level, and is slowly being affected by sea level rise. The first European contact was made in 1513 by the Spanish explorer Juan Ponce De Leon who named it "La Florida" meaning "Flowery Land." Before that, Florida was inhabited by native Indians, the most widely recognized tribes being the Seminole and Tequesta Indians.

The state Capitol is Tallahassee. The oldest city in the United States is St. Augustine, established in 1565 by Spain. Florida is home to the Everglades in South Florida, the Kennedy Space Center on Merritt Island, and Walt Disney World in Orlando. The climate of Florida varies from subtropical in the north to tropical in the south, and with an average daily temperature of 70.7 degrees Fahrenheit, it is the warmest state in the country. Due to the tropical climate Florida rarely receives snow. Florida is also known for its hurricane season that starts in June and ends in November. It is the lightning capital of the United States (here's hoping lightning really doesn't strike twice!) sometimes prone to afternoon thunderstorms.

After reading all of that, I decided that Florida was going to be a great adventure for me to discover. I especially liked the no snow part!

"Rayne, we are getting very close to our destination. Two more hours and your new life in Florida will officially begin." Uncle Bart's deep voice broke me out of my research mode. I turned off my iPad.

"Yes it will, uncle, thanks to you and Aunt Beth." I wanted them to know I was sincerely touched that they welcomed me into their family so warmly.

Aunt Beth reached for my hands clasping them tightly. "Your mom was right, Rayne, your life here will be an adventure, and sometimes, it will be a wildlife adventure too!"

Despite all the sadness in my heart from losing my mom, a slight feeling of curiosity mixed with excitement started to make me see the light at the end of a very dark tunnel. As I looked out the car window the warmth of the Florida sun started to make me drowsy. I fell asleep, and I didn't wake up until we arrived at the place I would now call home, The Homosassa Wildlife Park.

5: The Managers Residence

My Aunt Beth woke me up as we approached the Wildlife Park. The entrance to the park was marked by a majestic canopy of trees dripping with Spanish moss that enveloped us like a welcoming embrace.

"Those are Live Oak trees Rayne." My aunt explained. "They were planted decades ago. There are 11 on each side. Pretty cool, right?"

The road slightly curved as we exited the canopy of trees. My uncle took the very next right, turning down a road marked by a very cute manatee shaped mailbox and a sign that read "Wildlife Way." A bit further down the house I would now be living in revealed itself to me. I loved it immediately.

"This house was built in the 1960's by the original property owner of the Wildlife Park." My uncle informed me. "He built the house half Victorian, half Florida Cracker style, designing it to accommodate Florida's warm yet often wet environment."

The house was painted a soft shade of buttercup yellow and the first two stories were framed by large porches with ornate railings painted white. The top story was accented with double windows underlined with window boxes also painted white with colorful flowers brimming from them. One uniquely stunning aspect of the house was that it had the most vibrant dark pink flowers with forest green leaves climbing up the trellis on one whole side of the house.

"What are those flowers Uncle Bart? They are so pretty!" I asked.

"They are called Bougainvillea, Rayne, a plant you will see throughout the park, in many different colors. They thrive in Florida weather."

The front door opened and we were greeted by a woman with a welcoming smile. My cousin Aiden came rushing out like a mini tornado. "Mom! Dad!" He yelled as he jumped into Aunt Beth's arms. When he was done giving hugs to his mom and dad he turned shyly to me. "Hi" he softly said, unsure of what to do next. He was so sweet that I couldn't resist, I extended my arms to give him a hug.

"Hi Aiden, it's been a long time, but I hope we will become great friends!" I gave him a bear hug. His smile was huge.

"Me too, Rayne." he said. Suddenly his smile turned into a frown. "I'm sorry about your mom." He added, looking so forlorn I grabbed both his hands to hold them in mine.

"Thank you so much, Aiden, I appreciate you saying that."

My aunt introduced me to her friend Joni Greene who watched Aiden while my aunt and uncle came to Ohio to be with my mother and I in her final hours and to hold my mothers funeral. She greeted me warmly.

"Welcome to Florida Rayne, if you ever need anything I am here for you. I have two kids your age who are looking forward to meeting you once you get settled."

We entered the house and just like the outside, it was charming and inviting. The main floor was open and airy with wood flooring. A large fireplace was the main focal point in the living room. Aunt Beth told me the kitchen was also on the first floor at the back of the house. It had French doors that opened up to a backyard deck. She said they have lived there for four years, that it was the Park Managers residence.

Joni Greene said goodbye to all of us and Uncle Bart and Aiden walked her out so they could also unpack the car and bring my suitcases in. My mom and I had previously shipped some boxes of my belongings here in anticipation of my move, like bedding, books, and other personal items. Aunt Beth showed me the second floor where they had their bedrooms, bathrooms, and a study room, then showed me a small narrow staircase leading to the third floor. At the top of the stairs was a blue door.

"Through that door is your room Rayne, the whole top floor. As your mom already told you, it used to be a dormitory for interns coming to the wildlife park to study and work with the Florida wildlife, especially the manatees. As such, it is a mini apartment, and now it's all yours." Aunt Beth told me as she opened the door.

My eyes scanned the room taking it all in while I tried to absorb the fact that I would be living here. It was just like the pictures my mom showed me, but even better in person. The floors were a caramel colored wood, creaking softly beneath my feet. Straight ahead was a small kitchen, with its own refrigerator, sink, and stove. The bathroom was to the right, its door was open and I could see a claw footed white tub that had a cute light pink shower curtain attached to wrap around it for showering. Looking to the left I noticed a sitting area with an L-shaped sectional gray couch. It was accented with red pillows and had a soft looking red throw blanket draped on it. In front of the couch was a square shaped coffee table sitting upon a plush black rug I couldn't wait to put my feet on. There was even a nice T.V. stand with a large T.V. on it! Behind that, framed by weathered red brick walls, was the bedroom area. A queen sized bed with a black headboard was situated between two nightstands against the back brick wall. There was also a dresser with a mirror and a tall bookcase holding all of my beloved books. All of the furniture was made of wood painted a glossy black. I noticed my white Japanese inspired comforter decorated with small red and pink cherry blossoms on the bed. It was all so perfectly lovely! My favorite 3-D star shaped light was perched upon one of the nightstands while the other nightstand had a white orchid plant in a square black vase on it. This room was beyond amazing, I could not believe I could call it my own!

"What do you think, Rayne, do you like it?" Aunt Beth was curious to know. "I wanted you to feel comfortable from the time you walked in so I hope you don't mind that I started to decorate it for you. I think it turned out quite lovely, don't you?"

I looked at her and felt an unexpected surge of love.

"I love it so much, thank you, it's unbelievable! It's the warmest, coziest, best decorated room I have ever been in!" I claimed. I almost pinched myself it was so cool.

"Why don't you unwind a bit now while I get dinner ready. I'm sure you could use some time to yourself. Welcome home, Rayne."

She left and I sat on my new bed taking it all in. I thought of my mom and how much I missed her. I silently let her know that I was going to be alright, just as I promised her. For the first time I allowed myself to feel the excitement about my future here at the Homosassa Wildlife Park, my new home. My mom would be very proud.

6: Dinner with my new family

Uncle Bart brought my travel suitcases to my room so I spent the next hour putting my clothes in the dresser and other personal belongings in the side tables, placing my iPad dock, wifi wireless printer, and personal family photos on them. One of my favorite photos that I treasured more than anything else is a picture I have of my Dad with his arms wrapped around my mother, who is holding me, a very chubby and happy baby, in her arms. Everyone has a big smile on their face. It is a photo that shows what a true happy family looks like. I put that special framed photo prominently on the table to the left of my bed, where it could be viewed no matter where you stood in the large room. I'm slightly obsessive about organization and cleanliness. In my world, everything has a place, I just can't relax in my room unless its clean and orderly. Looking around my new living arrangement I once again could not believe that it was going to be all mine. I am going to enjoy keeping it nice and would appreciate staying here for however long. When I finished unpacking I went downstairs to see if I could help my aunt with dinner. I have always loved to cook, my mom taught me about the importance of being able to make a nice meal using fresh and healthy ingredients and making them taste great with seasonings. Upon entering the kitchen I was greeted with the most pleasant smelling aroma surrounding me, causing my stomach to immediately grumble. It made me realize that I was positively ravenous!

"What is that you're making, Aunt Beth? It smells wonderful!"

"It's called Grouper Buerre Blanc, Rayne. It is baked Black Grouper filet topped with a lemon butter caper white wine sauce. Your mom told me you loved seafood so I wanted you to experience what is popular to eat here locally. We love to eat fish like the black grouper we are having now, as well as Florida red snapper, and if you're very lucky and it's in season, the highly prized snook fish. I would love to show you how easy it is to make some time soon, if you'd like."

I told her I would and I thought a fish called "snook" sounded very weird, but it was obviously tasty by her explanation.

"Thank you, Aunt Beth, I'm hungry and you're so thoughtful. I can't wait to try it!" I felt very flattered that she went to so much trouble on my behalf, and after I tried the grouper, I was blown away---it was SO GOOD! Grouper is a mild and moist, pleasant tasting fish and the delicate cream sauce topping was buttery silky with a slight tang from the fresh lemon and tiny bits of pickled capers. It was an explosion of great tasting flavors! She served this with steamed broccoli and soft buttered croissants. Aiden declared his mom a great chef, I agreed. During our dinner Uncle Bart talked about the wildlife park. He told me about the large freshwater spring cove leading out into the crystal clear blue waters of the Homosassa River, which in turn leads to the Gulf of Mexico. He explained that the park, situated by that spring, was home to an underwater observatory, a one of a kind underwater observation station with huge plexi-glass widows designed to view the marine life in its own environment under the water. It is also home to a large variety of Florida wildlife and is the only natural habitat for the West Indian Manatee in a captive environment, as they can roam around the large and pristine spring waters freely, yet are kept from leaving by a metal fence under the water. The fence has metal bars that are a foot wide apart, not wide enough for the Manatee to slip through, yet accommodating enough for the fish to swim through. It was topped by a 30 ft. long bridge. When the time comes for a manatee to be released back into the wild, they lift the hydraulic gate and off they go, into the Homosassa river and beyond to the Gulf.

"I am very proud of the parks rehabilitation program for sick or injured manatee's in need of state of the art current medical facilities." He proudly claimed.

"As you should be." my aunt continued. "It's a sanctuary for them to rest and recover before being released back out to their native habitat as soon as possible. Just a few manatee are there permanently and only when they have long term handicaps."

I made a mental note to look up the facts about the manatee very soon.

"Manatee are called gentle giants, Rayne, and that is exactly what they are." Uncle Bart said with a smile. "They are friendly, loving, inquisitive marine mammals with a very unique shape. As a Junior Wildlife Ranger, you will be responsible for helping to take care of them, making diets, observing behavior, and educating the visitors at the park about them. I think you will enjoy it."

"I know I will Uncle Bart. When can I start?"

"The Jr. Ranger Wildlife Academy begins on Monday. You will have time this weekend to meet the other residents your age who live here, they have already signed up for the program. I know them well, they are great kids who love working with animals, just as I know you will. So rest up you have a very busy week ahead of you."

And just like that my first dinner in Florida was over.

7: The Sanctuary

I was literally jumping out of my skin with a strong desire to start exploring the park, but for now I would have to be content with exploring the backyard nature of my new home with Aiden leading as the tour guide. After dinner we walked down a winding path surrounded by tall trees and dense brush leading to the river. Uncle Bart set forth some rules before we left, and as I walked with Aiden through the vast and brilliantly colored different shades of green I recalled his words.

"I'm not a strict man, Rayne, the only rules I have for you living here are rules that will keep you safe at all times, rules that I feel are necessary to guide you in life. One rule that I feel is very important is this-always be aware of your environment, and respect all wildlife from a distance. This park is a nature preserve, you will see wildlife like deer, armadillos, raccoons, too many birds to mention. Wildlife in Florida is much more diverse than in Ohio, so many different species of animals thrive living here because the climate is so tropical and the food sources are endless. The wildlife I want you to be on the constant look out for at all times when walking around here are the reptilian kind, snakes. It is a very real possibility for you to get a glimpse of some kind of snake. Most of them are harmless, like the Corn snakes and the Black Racer. There are some that are venomous however, the Rattlesnakes, Water Moccasins, and the Coral snake. They will not bother you, unless you step directly on them. Stick to the paths and you may never see them. But if you do, stop and back away immediately. I don't want to alarm you, I just want to educate you about what wildlife exists here."

I never thought about the danger of living at a Wildlife Park. I assured him I would abide by that rule, most definitely!

I asked Aiden during our walk if he ever saw a snake on this path.

"I saw a venomous Coral snake sunning itself in our backyard once. I wasn't sure at first because there is another snake that looks just like it called the Scarlet King snake which is not venomous and completely harmless. They both have a red, black, and yellow scale pattern."

He told me a cool way to tell the two apart.

"If the red touches black, it's a friend of Jack. If the red touches yellow, it can kill a fellow. That's how I knew it was a Coral snake, because the red was next to the yellow! I stayed far away from it. It was pretty though. The park has both of those species of snake displayed in the Reptile House, you will see the difference for yourself."

I was eager to learn about all the wildlife living here, including the reptilian kind. As soon as I finished that thought we came upon the river and it was a sight to behold, so beautiful I was momentarily stunned into silence. What I saw ahead of me was a huge slice of Florida paradise.

8: Dock encounters of the unusual kind

Aiden grabbed my hand and we ran to the large dock made of wood. We sat down on the dock, dangling our feet over the water, taking in the beauty before us. My senses were all heightened, hearing, sight, smell. The smell of the earth meeting water meeting pure air was so intoxicating, I could almost taste it. This was a place of zen, and I needed some zen very badly. I briefly closed my eyes for a minute to meditate when all of a sudden a strange sound came from the water behind me, startling me so much it caused me to jump up quickly! It sounded like something was gasping for air while spouting water up at the same time--- was that even possible? And what the heck was it???

"Look Rayne!" Aiden pointed to the water. "It's a manatee with her calf who just came up for a breath of air! They are slowly going back down, but will come up again very soon. She can stay underwater for up to twenty minutes at a time but she might not wait that long. They are just as curious about us as we are them."

I went closer to where Aiden stood on the deck so I could look where he was excitingly pointing. I could see them clearly in the water close by. Come up please, I wished, let me see you better! I knew one thing, I wasn't going anywhere until she did! After a few long minutes, I noticed her making her way up, followed by the baby, 'a calf' according to Aiden. When they reached the top I could see their adorable pudgy faces up close, and they had wide spaced black button eyes above a triangular shaped snout.

Aiden got down on his knees and tapped the water with his hands.

"If she comes to me I can gently touch her, but it's illegal to harass a manatee and chase them. They have to come to you."

I watched him with the mother manatee who was gliding slowly next to the dock. She stopped to nuzzle Aidens hand with her mouth, surrounded by what appeared to be whiskers. Manatees have whiskers!

"Can she bite you Aiden? Would she?"

"No, manatees are friendly, they don't bite. They do have teeth, molars, toward the back of their mouths, but you can't see them unless you feed them. I think they like their whiskers rubbed. Do you see her scars on her back? She has three large slashes along her back, she must of been previously hit by a boat propeller. She also has another scar over there. Unfortunately manatees are too slow to avoid a speeding boat."

I joined Aiden by getting on my knees and putting out my hand.

"It looks like a rose almost, the other scar." I said to Aiden. To my utter amazement the mother manatee allowed me to scratch her back-not moving while I did it! Her skin reminded me of an elephant's skin, even the color was similar to an elephants. She liked her back rub so much she rolled over to expose her belly to me, she actually 'grabbed' my hand with her flippers to keep me rubbing her! I laughed out loud in delight for the first time in months when she did that-how could I not? I did this for a few minutes before she started to swim away, her calf following her, leaving me astonished that I had just had this amazing encounter.

"That is one of the most incredible moments I have ever experienced, Aiden, thanks so much for bringing me here. I think I just fell in love for the first time!"

"Me too." I heard a male voice from behind us, startling me once again. I turned around to find myself facing what had to be the best looking boy on this planet-and he was looking directly at me.

9: Maverick and the Injured Pelican

He was sitting in a red Kayak with what appeared to be a portable pet carrier next to him. I was so mesmerized by the manatee I never heard him coming!

"Hey Maverick!" Aiden greeted him enthusiastically. "Need some help?"

I was glad Aiden could talk because for the moment I was dumbstruck. I could feel my cheeks getting warm. I wondered for the first time if this is what blushing felt like.

"Hey buddy, yes I do. Can you grab the carrier for me while I get the kayak tied up?" Maverick replied.

"Sure thing, Maverick!" Aiden said as he went to grab the carrier. "Rayne, this is Maverick Greene. You met his mom earlier, they live here on property too. His mom is the Wildlife Supervisor and he has a twin sister named Mallory. Maverick, this is Rayne, my cousin who now lives with us."

"Nice to meet you Rayne, we heard you were coming. My sister is going to be so mad I got to meet you first. Welcome to Florida."

"Nice to meet you too." I somehow managed to say, all the while wondering why I suddenly felt so shy. I followed Aiden to help him lift the large pet carrier up on to the dock for Maverick who was effortlessly jumping out of the Kayak to climb up to the dock. He was tall and slender yet muscular, his skin caramelized by the sun. I noticed his medium length, slightly curly, sun streaked brown hair was naturally highlighted with light brown and blonde shades-he obviously spends a lot of time outside enjoying the Florida sun. His hair was tied back yet was still slightly wild and untamed, and when he put his shirt on some of his hair fell down around his face attractively.

For some strange reason I found myself wanting to reach out and touch it. I almost reached out to do exactly that when thankfully I was immediately distracted by looking at his eyes. Oh-my-goodness his eyes! To my utter surprise Maverick's eyes were each a different color-one was light green-the other bright blue-both the color of the Sea! I'd never seen that before, and I couldn't help but stare. Our eyes connected and for me the world stopped for one moment right then and there, I was completely mesmerized not just by the color of his eyes but by the intensity of them looking directly into mine. It was powerful yet confounding at the same time! I always wondered what it would be like to be hypnotized, surely it was like this. His dark eyebrows framing those gorgeous eyes raised slightly conveying self confidence, amusement, and curiosity all combined. If that wasn't potent enough, his strong jaw was marked with a small dent. I reluctantly pulled my eyes away from his. I was kind of blown away by these feelings, yet I was extremely curious to know what was in the carrier, I couldn't tell because the front of the carrier had a covering over it.

"What is in here, Maverick?" Aiden asked looking at the carrier. Apparently he was curious too.

"It's an injured pelican, the Wildlife Department got a call from the Monkey Bar restaurant saying it needed rescued. It has an injury from a fish hook and had monofilament wrapped around one of its wings. I managed to extract the monofilament but unfortunately the fish hook damaged the pelicans throat pouch, which now has a huge hole in it. When it tries to eat fish they fall right out of the pouch before they can be swallowed. I'm taking it to the Wildlife Hospital so they can fix it. It wasn't hard to catch, so it's probably weak and hungry."

Why wasn't I surprised that Mr. Really Cute was also a Wildlife Hero? I couldn't help but smile.

"Fascinating." Maverick said under his breath but I still heard him. "Why the smile, Rayne?"

For a moment I didn't think I was going to be able to answer him, I couldn't let him know what I was actually thinking so I quickly thought of something else to say.

"I'm thinking that it's wonderful you rescued the pelican." I heard myself reply. I was so glad I was able to get that out. Honestly, what the heck was wrong with me? Why was I finding it so hard to communicate with him? Maverick smiled back at me and continued.

"Thank you both for your help. Come by the Wildlife Hospital some time soon so you can see for yourself how the pelican gets treatment. I hope you will?" He said to me. I felt myself blushing brightly once again.

"O.K. Maverick, see you later!" My adorable cousin told him. We watched Mr. Really Cute jog away with the injured pelican. Again, I said nothing. Why didn't I say nice to meet you or something normal like that? **#Ugh**. I decided my problem was that I was mentally exhausted, because it had been a very long day. At least, that's what I told myself. I never had a problem talking to anyone before, ever.

"Let's go home, Aiden." I said, glancing back once more at the dock on the river. "Again, thanks for bringing me here. I love it."

"You're welcome Rayne. I'm glad you got to meet Maverick, I really like him. He's so cool!"

I silently agreed. We walked back to the house and when we got there I said goodnight to everyone. I could not wait to see what the next day would bring, but for now, I was really tired. After a hot bath I fell asleep thinking about manatees, the injured pelican, and Mavericks green/blue eyes. I slept soundly.

10: New Friendships

Iwoke up early the next morning thinking about my mom, wishing I could talk to her, wishing I could hug her. The physical pain of sorrow really packs a powerful punch! I know I promised her I would be strong, but I also know she would forgive me for crying once again for the thousandth time over losing her. After wiping away my somewhat therapeutic tears I decided to get my iPad to read something she wrote to me. I went to the Notes application and read another letter.

"Friendships"

Sometimes Me Think,

"What is Friend?"

And then me say,

"Friend is someone to share the last cookie with"

- Cookie Monster, Sesame Street

Hello my dearest daughter. Let me start with telling you how much I love and adore you! I wanted to start this letter about friendship with a little humor, as we both know you have loved the Cookie Monster since you were two. On a serious note, no one knows you better than me and I think anyone would be lucky to call you their friend. You are kind, loyal, and empathetic, three very admiral traits a person can have. Throughout your life you will meet many different people, and each person will be unique. The common thread we humans share is our character. Are you a good person? Are you trustworthy? Are you loyal? I think a true friend is hard to come by and as such, should be treasured. You can have many acquaintances, but only a few really good, lifelong friends. Keep yourself open to new friendships, so when you find a friend you can trust with your innermost feelings and secrets~let them know you can offer the same. Just know that you don't need someone to complete you, you only need someone to accept you completely. Finally, don't be friends with negative people, they will only bring you down. Life is too short as we both know to waste time on people who don't deserve your goodness. Unfortunately, some people are just not happy, or kind. Stay away from them. Have fun meeting new friends, Rayne, and if you find someone you really enjoy spending time with that has your back no matter what~work hard to keep that friend. Share that last cookie with them.

I finished her note and was glad I read it. It gave me a surge of strength I desperately needed to get up and start my day. I put on white shorts with one of my favorite white cotton T-shirts that had a picture of a pink unicorn on it stating "Stay Magical." I figured it would help my mood improve to wear such an amusing yet comfortable shirt, looking at it always makes me smile and I could use all the magic and positive vibes I could get to help bring me out of the relentlessly sad funk I was dwelling in. I went downstairs to see what the day would bring. Aunt Beth was sitting on the porch in one of the comfy looking black rocking chairs drinking coffee. She told me the boys were out fishing and asked me what I liked to drink in the morning, I told her I loved hot green tea with honey. We went in the house to make some and then came back out to sit down together. After sipping our morning drinks for a few minutes in silence and taking in the tranquil shift of cool morning Florida sunbeams turning warmer and brighter, my aunt brought up something I was eager to hear about.

"Let's talk about Wildlife Ranger Academy, Rayne. I am a part of the Jr. Ranger program, it's something I love to do. As you already know I am the Education Director at the park. I will help you learn about the park and animals. Bart will take you every morning to the Academy on his way to work. We need to stock up your refrigerator with breakfast goods and snacks, as well as drinks, so you don't miss breakfast. We also have to go shopping for some shoes and shorts that you will need as a Wildlife Ranger. You will be given a shirt, hat, and a wetsuit for when you have to go in the water. Most of the kids wear cargo shorts and timberland boots. We can go later if you like?"

"I'd love to, Aunt Beth, sounds great." I replied. I hadn't even thought about a uniform, so I was glad she did. Just as we finished that conversation two girls came walking up our driveway. One of the girls was petite with light blonde beach wavy hair, the other was much taller and her hair was the color of cinnamon, with chunky light brown and auburn highlights pulled back into two perfectly styled French braids. When she came closer I noticed her hair matched the color of her eyes. My aunt introduced us.

"Hello girls, I'd like to introduce you to my niece, Rayne Lanecastor!"

"Hello Mrs. Kane! Hello Rayne!" The petite girl beamed. Her smile was wide and engaging, I could see she wore braces, the clear kind. The resemblance to Maverick was pretty obvious, but I wondered, could this be Mallory, Maverick's twin sister?

"Top of the morning to you, Mallory." My Aunt Beth greeted her, answering my question.

"And same to you, Jenzy. It's good to see you both. Why don't you girls go up to Rayne's room and get to know each other? I'll bring up some freshly squeezed Florida orange juice and Krispy Kreme doughnuts that Bart got this morning."

"Thank you Aunt Beth. What's a 'Krispy Kreme' donut?" I was curious to know.

"Krispy Kreme donuts are the BEST, most DELICIOUS donuts on the Planet Earth! They're positively addicting!" Mallory claimed.

I looked at the girls and smiled. "Well then, I can't wait to try one! I'm so happy to meet you both, would you like to see my room?"

"Oh my goodness YESSSSSSS!" Mallory drawled. "Show us the way!"

I looked at Jenzy nodding her head yes too so I led them upstairs. I was a little nervous, but more excited. New friendships here I come!

11: Mallory & Jenzy

"**T**his room is *BA-NA-NAS*!!!" Mallory declared.

I couldn't help but laugh at the way she said it. I was beginning to realize that getting to know Mallory would be a lot of fun.

"It is pretty great." I agreed. "Straight ahead is the kitchen and the bathroom is to the right. To the left is the lounge area, behind that is where I sleep. Please make yourselves comfortable."

"Thank you, Rayne, your room rocks. Though it's more like a small apartment than a room." Jenzy finally said. She walked over to my nightstand in the bedroom area and picked up my family photo. I followed her there, suddenly feeling anxious, wondering what I'd say about the loss of my parents. Turned out I didn't have to say anything.

"We know you recently lost your mom, and your dad when you were little. Quite honestly, Mallory and I wondered what to say to you. We decided we would just say how sorry we were to hear it, and that we hoped we could all become good friends. You know, looking at this picture, I see so much love." She gingerly put my treasured photo back down and looked at me with the most genuine smile. I knew right then and there that we would become the best of friends.

Aunt Beth brought in the donuts.

"Enjoy girls! Just so you know, that couch converts to a bed, so if you'd like to have a sleepover next weekend, I'm all for it. Rayne, in a couple hours we will go shopping O.K?" She asked.

"Yes, thank you Aunt Beth."

When she left Mallory, Jenzy, and I sat in the 'lounge.' (I liked saying that better than living room, not sure why) we dug into the donuts and Mallory was right, it was the best tasting, most delicious donut I had ever tasted! It melted in my mouth, it was so sugary good. The donut I was falling fast in love with was a raspberry filled glazed donut. At first bite, I experienced food nirvana. This Krispy Kreme donut was the best thing I ever tasted! **#KrispyKremeFanForLife!**

We ate the first donut in rapturous silence, then Mallory spoke up.

"Why don't we get to know each other better? We could take turns talking about ourselves to become better acquainted. I'll be happy to start."

"Go for it!" Jenzy said.

"Yes, please." I grabbed a second scrumptious donut while giving her my full attention.

"My full name is Mallory Marie Greene. I have a twin brother named Maverick, who I heard you already met~yes?" She questioned in my direction. I nodded affirmatively.

"We are both 15, almost 16, and my mother-who you have also met, has been the Wildlife Supervisor for the park for two years now. She is also a Veterinarian, my brother and I have grown up around all kinds of animals, domestic and wild. He wants to be a Marine Biologist, I want to be a Vet like my mom. I have a cat named Jaguar that I love dearly, she has kittens that are almost two months old. Maverick and I rescued her, when my mom gave her a health examination we discovered that she was not only abandoned, she was pregnant as well. On a more serious note, my dad lives in South Florida-I rarely see him. My parents divorced four years ago, it's for the best. He moved soon after. He's remarried and I hardly ever see him. It sucks but --I've learned to deal with it. My favorite color is red and I love, love, love Vintage thrift stores! My favorite thing to do besides working with animals is to go paddle boarding. One of the best aspects of living at the park is having access to kayaks and paddle boards to use after the park is closed for the day. Have you ever tried paddle boarding, Rayne?"

"No I haven't, But I would like very much to learn how to use a paddle board, as well as a kayak. They both look like so much fun!"

"They are, I will be happy to teach you how to do both!" Mallory's grin was infectious. "That's just about it, except I do admit to having a serious addiction to gummy bears, but I have to take out my Invisalign braces to eat them! Your turn, Jenzy!"

"It's kind of hard to compete with gummy bears but I will give it my best shot!" Jenzy laughed and proceeded from there. "My full name is Jenzy Jackson, no middle name. My dad is the Assistant Park Manager here at the park. Rayne, your Uncle Bart hired my dad, they are very good friends. My mom works part time at the library, which is great because I really enjoy reading. If I wasn't going to work with animals I would be a Stylist, I'm really good at applying makeup and fixing hair. By the way, Mallory, Maverick described Rayne's hair color perfectly, didn't he? He said it was like rose gold, and it is. It's quite pretty, Rayne, the perfect length for braiding too. May I braid it sometime?"

I think I answered 'sure' but I was still trying to absorb the fact the Maverick noticed the color of my hair! Why was I secretly happy about that?

Jenzy continued. "I love caramel Milky Way candy bars and Dr. Pepper. My favorite animal is the manatee, but I can't wait to start learning more about reptiles. I love Japanese Anime, and I am a huge fan of Sonic the hedgehog. That just about sums me up but there is one more thing you should know about me. My addictions are my iPhone and makeup so I babysit kids, pets, and fish anytime someone will hire me to help pay for my phone services and makeup purchases. So, you've heard all about Mallory and myself, Rayne, now it's your turn to tell us all about you."

My turn. "My full name is Rayne Elissa Lanecastor, I am 15 years old. Elissa was my moms name. I was born in Cleveland, Ohio, home to the Rock and Roll Hall of Fame and the Cleveland Indians. My favorite animals are dolphins, Orcas, and lemurs. I enjoy putting together different craft projects and baking desserts like Macarons which are very challenging to make correctly. I love to download any music from the eighties, Like REO Speedwagon, Journey, Styx, Run DMC, the Cure, and especially Queen and Freddie Mercury! My favorite possession is my Apple iPad that my mother gave to me before she died. I get your addiction to technology Jenzy, I'm right there with you! I love cherry tootsie roll pops, Sprite, and Japanese candy. I also now *LOVE* Krispy Kreme donuts! (We all laughed at that.) Last, but not least, I am thrilled to get to know you both-hopefully we can become forever friends." That's all I could think of to say.

The room was quiet for a minute before Mallory stood up and said "I second that!"

Jenzy concurred, also standing up. "Me too!"

"Me three!" I stood up as well, and we all shook on it with sticky glazed donut hands.

And so our friendships began.

12: Preparing for the Wildlife Academy

Before my new friends left to go home we made plans to have a slumber party the next weekend and meet early in the morning to start the Wildlife Academy. We were curious to meet the other participants who signed up, there were 8 of us in total. I told my Aunt Beth about the slumber party plans as we were shopping at the Crystal River Mall later that afternoon. I could tell she was pleased I enjoyed my time with them.

"I knew you'd click with Mallory & Jenzy." She smiled at me. "They are terrific girls. Mallory's mom is one of my best friends. She is a woman I admire greatly as a mom and as a friend."

A couple hours later we completed a successful shopping trip at the mall. I was now a proud owner of a brand new pair of waterproof dark green Timberland boots, Khaki colored cargo shorts, and a S'well water bottle that was kind of expensive but claimed to keep water cold for up to 48 hours. My Aunt Beth said that the most important thing to do at the Academy was to keep well hydrated by drinking tons of water. The summers in Florida are brutal, and it is easy to suffer from heatstroke.

"In Florida, the temperature's can be in the 90's but add in the humidity factor and it will feel like it is in the 100's. It's no joke, recently the high temperatures have reached record levels."

After the mall we went grocery shopping at the Publix grocery store located down the street from the Wildlife Park. I picked up my very favorite breakfast foods; bagels, blueberries, bananas, (*BA-NA-NAS*! as Mallory would say) granola, and organic French Vanilla yogurt. I also purchased green tea, honey, milk, and coconut water as well as sugar and butter. My Aunt Beth explained to me that my mom designated a credit card for me to use for food and necessities, but that I would not have to use it for groceries as they would take care of that. I already knew my mom had formed a trust for me, to pay for college and for whatever I needed in the future. There was also a decent amount earmarked for my future wedding that I had cried about that crazy day so long ago when my life flashed before my eyes-a wedding I still couldn't imagine having even now. My mom's wish was for me to get a college education then find work that I would love to do. I am going to proudly honor that wish. I felt very grown up picking out my own groceries and stocking the refrigerator in my kitchen when we were done with shopping. While I was putting the groceries away I saw my mom's well used waffle making machine tucked away in a cabinet. I was glad to see it made the trip from Ohio still in one piece. It made me happy to see it, it's the little things in life that bring the most comfort. Making waffles together was something my mom and I used to do at least once a week. Homemade Belgian waffles are delicious. I decided to get the ingredients later this week to make them the morning after the sleepover. I was really looking forward to the sleepover but first, I had to get through my first week at the Wildlife Academy. I took a shower and put together my outfit for the next day, cargo shorts with a white V neck cotton t-shirt paired with my new Timberlands. I added an army green canvas satchel I already owned that was roomy enough to carry my iPad, a couple of notebooks and folders. When I finished I still had some time to kill before dinner with my new family so I got my iPad to search the manatee, taking the time to print out any information I liked with my wi-fi printer. Technology is seriously cool, just like the manatee. I got some great information from the internet and the Save the Manatee Club. I decided to make a folder for wildlife information, starting with the manatee.

Florida Manatee

Scientific classification

Kingdom: Animalia

Phylum: Chordata

Class: Mammalia

Infraclass: Eutheria

Order: Sirenia

Family: Trichechidae

Genus: Trichechus

Manatees are large, aquatic, and herbivorous marine mammals. They are nicknamed "Sea Cows" or "Gentle Giants." Three species of the manatee exist, the Amazonian manatee, the West Indian manatee, and the West African manatee. Manatees comprise three of the four living species in the order Sirenia. The fourth is the eastern hemisphere's Dugong. The closest living land relative to the manatee is the Elephant.

Description

Manatees are large, aquatic mammals with bodies that taper to a flat, paddle shaped tail. They have two forelimbs, called flippers, with three to four nails on each flipper. The color of their skin is grey, and it is thick and coarse. They can weigh between 880-1200 pounds and reach a length of up to 12 feet. Females manatees are usually larger and heavier. They have a large, flexible, prehensile upper lip dotted by whiskers and a small snout. They use the lip to gather their food to eat, as well as using it for socialization and communication. Adult manatee do not have incisor or canine teeth, but possess a set of just six molars in each jaw toward the back of its mouth. They have small, widely spaced, button shaped eyes and nostrils and because they are mammals they must surface every 3-5 minutes on average to breath air. When resting however, they are known to stay submerged for up to twenty minutes.

Reproduction

Manatees are not sexually mature until they are about five years old. They breed once every two years, with a gestation period of 12 months. They nurse their young for 12-18 months, during which time the calf is dependent upon its mother. It is believed that one calf is born every two to five years, and twins are rare.

Diet

Manatees are herbivores and eat aquatic plants and are the only plant eating marine mammals. They can eat both saltwater (Seagrasses, marine algae , turtle grass) and freshwater plants (alligator weed, floating hyacinth, hydrilla, water lettuce). they use their front flippers and large, flexible lips to manipulate vegetation. They will eat up to 5-10 percent of their body weight in vegetation per day. Both the West Indian and West African manatees may require a source of fresh water to consume and most scientists agree that manatees must have access to fresh water.

Habitat and Range

Manatees can be found in shallow, slow moving rivers, estuaries, saltwater bays, canals, and coastal areas, particularly where seagrass beds or freshwater vegetation flourish. They are a migratory species. Manatees inhabit the shallow, marshy coastal areas and rivers of the Caribbean Sea and the Gulf of Mexico, (West Indian manatee) the Amazon Basin, (Amazonian manatee) and West Africa (West African manatee). West Indian Manatees enjoy warmer waters and are known to congregate in shallow waters. They cannot survive below 15*C (60*F). Their natural source for warmth is warm, spring-fed rivers. Within the United States they are concentrated in Florida in the winter.

*Side note-The West Indian manatee migrates into Florida rivers, such as the Homosassa, Crystal, and the Chassahowitzka Rivers. The head springs of these rivers maintain a 22*C (72*) temperature year round. During November to March, approximately 400 West Indian manatees congregate in the rivers in Citrus County, Florida.

Lifespan and Mortality

Manatees have no natural enemies, and it is believed they can live for up to 60 years or more. As with all wild animal populations, a percentage of manatee mortality is attributed to natural causes of death, such as cold stress, gastrointestinal disease, pneumonia, and other diseases. A high number of additional fatalities occur from human-related causes, such as collisions with watercrafts. (Boats). Other causes from human-related manatee mortality include being crushed and/or drowned in canal locks and flood control structures; ingestion of fish hooks, litter, and monofila-ment line; and entanglement in crab trap lines. Ultimately, loss of habitat is the most serious threat facing Manatees in the United States today.

Legal Protection

West Indian manatees in the United States are protected under federal law by the Marine Mammal Protection Act of 1972, and the Endangered Specie Act of 1973, which makes it illegal to harass, hunt, capture, or kill any marine mammal. West Indian manatees are also protected by the Florida Manatee Sanctuary Act of 1978. Violations of the Federal or State laws can be met with civil or criminal convictions associated with monetary fines and/or imprisonment.

I absorbed the information about the manatee, the gentle giants, deciding it wasn't always easy being a manatee. I printed out the information then put it in a 3-ring binder I had found in my book case that I had never used. I labeled it **"Wildlife Information."** I was putting the binder in my satchel when I heard a knock at my door. It was my Uncle Bart.

"Hi Rayne can I come in for a minute and talk?"

"Yes of course."

"I'm here to talk to you about tomorrow. The Wildlife Academy begins at 7 in the morning. The Wildlife Rangers arrive at the same time to get the park ready for opening. The first week of the Academy for Junior Rangers is spent learning about zoo-keeping practices and learning about the wildlife residing at the park. I postponed the date of the Academy by two weeks when I found out you would be participating. I wanted you to be part of it from the very beginning. We haven't had a chance to explore the park so I'd love to show you around after you are done for the day. The main mode of transportation around the park is by energy efficient golf carts, as Park Manager I have my own. Are you interested?" He questioned.

"Absolutely Uncle Bart, I'd love it!" I answered.

"It's settled then. Be downstairs at 6:45 in the morning and I will drop you off at the Wildlife Building before I go to my office. I will pick you up again at 2 in the afternoon to give you a tour. On the first day of the Academy the park volunteers buy pizza for the new rangers for lunch, so all the Junior Rangers can get to know each other better. After tomorrow you can spend your lunch break eating at home or at the Wildlife Park's cafe. The food is really good there. Any questions?"

"No Sir, but I'd like to tell you thank you again, I am so appreciative about everything you and Aunt Beth are doing for me."

I thought I was going to start crying, so I stopped there.

My Uncle Bart came over to me pulling me into a welcoming hug.

"I loved your mom and dad very much, Rayne, as I love you. You honor me by joining my family. You are family forever. You never owe us thanks, WE owe you the thanks."

As he let me go I saw he had tears in his eyes. I knew right then that I was no longer a pathetically sad orphan, I was loved, I had a new family. And I was home.

13: The Wildlife Academy

It was still dark when my alarm went off the next morning. I turned on my bedside lamp while regretfully exiting my warm cocoon. I could feel butterflies in my stomach so I made some hot tea to calm my nerves. While I drank it I looked at my iPad to see all the notes my mom left me. I noticed one titled "Conquer your fears, and you'll conquer the World."

How appropriate. I clicked on to it.

"Conquer your fears, and you will conquer the World"

Franklin D. Roosevelt once said, 'The only thing we have to fear is fear itself' and I agree. Fear is an emotion that we all feel as humans at one time or another, usually about the unknown. It's an unpleasant emotion to be sure but it is natural to be nervous about the unexpected or to fear something you don't like. For every person it's different: it could be a fear of spiders, public speaking, or perhaps a fear of heights. Fear can be paralyzing, literally, for some people. You should know that everybody is afraid of something. So how do you conquer your fears? I believe you do it with courage. Recognize that you are not alone with feeling some type of fear, it's normal. What I want for you my love, is to understand that it's ok to feel it, but not be paralyzed by it.

If you think positive, the outcome will be positive. Take a deep breath, calm your nerves, and tackle whatever fear you may have head on! Live your life to the fullest. Love, Mom.

I pondered this over for a few minutes while making myself a toasted bagel with butter for breakfast. I would now keep in mind that I probably wasn't the only one nervous about the first day of the Wildlife Academy. I finished my bagel then cruised downstairs to start my day, my "butterflies" now almost completely gone.

"Good Morning Rayne." Uncle Bart greeted me warmly. "Are you ready to go?"

We walked outside to his golf cart. How fun! I never rode in a golf cart before but I liked it. It made perfect sense that they would be the main mode of transportation at the park. He drove me to the Wildlife Building and as we approached I saw Mallory and Jenzy waving at me with smiles on their faces.

"I see I'm leaving you in good hands." He waved back hello to the girls. "Have a great day. I will pick you up here at 2 for your tour."

"Goodbye for now, uncle!" I said jumping off the golf cart when he stopped so I could join my new friends. Mallory motioned for me to sit next to them on the stairs leading up to the building.

"My mom is going to give us a tour of the Wildlife Building then tell us all about the Junior Ranger program." Mallory let me know. "I know the building well, it's incredible!"

"Here comes Maverick and Drew McArthur now." Jenzy pointed out.

"Drew is super chill and super charming. Wait until you hear his accent." Mallory gazed in his direction with more than a hint of admiration.

Maverick grinned broadly when he saw me. The butterflies in my stomach came back full force, but this time in a *good* way.

"Hi ladies, good morning! Are you ready to conquer the wildlife world?" He questioned with a killer smile that was contagious. "Rayne, this is my new friend Drew, he's from South Africa. He is interning here at the park for the summer."

"Hello Drew, pleasure to meet you." I extended my hand to his. You know the saying 'Tall, dark, and handsome?' Yep. That's Drew McArthur. Tall, with skin the color of night and copper-hued brown eyes so striking I struggled to come up with an accurate description of their color. Wow, I thought, I hadn't been in Florida one week and I had already met two of the cutest guys I had ever seen.

"The pleasure is mine, Rayne." Instead of shaking my hand, he grabbed me into a bear hug! "That's how we greet in South Africa!"

I glanced over at Maverick. Was that a flash of annoyance I saw in his eyes?

"And good day to two other great girls!" Drew released me then bear hugged Jenzy and Mallory.

"Well aren't you quite the charmer!" Mallory giggled.

"Good Morning, Drew, are you getting comfortable in your new surroundings?" Jenzy asked.

"I am, Jenzy." He replied.

"Drew is 17 and is interning at the park to study manatees for the summer." Mallory explained. "My mom is responsible for watching over his well-being while he is here. He is living in one of the new intern rooms in the Wildlife Building . He is also attending the Academy, along with one other intern staying at the park. Speaking of which, here she comes now." Mallory said, her good mood suddenly disappearing.

I looked up to see a girl walking out of the Wildlife Building so cool and serene I could not take my eyes off her. She commanded attention, and she got it. You know when someone is so captivating that everyone around them stops doing what they are doing to stare? She was *that* someone. Her black hair shimmered in the morning sun and was parted in the middle then pulled back into a sleek ponytail reaching halfway down her back like liquid silk. As she glided toward us I could see she had light brown eyes framed by two perfectly arched brows and full lips enhanced with red lipstick. She greeted the boys (completely ignoring us girls, btw) saying, "Buenos días amigos! Am I late for this very important date?" She spoke with a spanish accent that was far more silky than her hair.

"Clearly not, Serafina, we are waiting on my mom and three others to get here, so you're right on time." Mallory replied, looking like she just tasted a sour patch candy. I wondered why, making a mental note to ask her later when we were alone.

Maverick introduced us. "Rayne, this is Serafina Serrano, the other intern staying at the park to study manatees for the summer. My mom is chaperoning her as well. You have to be at least 16 to be an intern. She's from Miami."

"Hi Serafina! I'm Rayne Lanecastor, nice to meet you." I offered her my hand to shake, which she ignored. **#awkward**! I lamely dropped my hand as quickly as I could.

"Hello." She said, immediately dismissing me. She turned to Drew and purred, "Darling, you played your music too loud last night, I barely got the beauty sleep I needed! My room is across the way from yours, remember?" She pouted prettily.

"My apologies Serafina, I will try to be more quiet in the future." He promised.

Mallory and Mavericks mom joined us with the other kids attending the wildlife academy, asking us to all gather around.

"Hello Junior Wildlife Rangers, I'm Joni Greene, it's nice to meet all of you. I'm the Wildlife Supervisor, your new boss. Thank you for being on time, that is one of the most important traits you must have to be a Junior Ranger. The animals here deserve punctuality. We will begin the Wildlife Academy with a tour of the Wildlife Building , a place I am very proud of. Are you ready?" She asked us. We all nodded our heads in unison. "Then let's begin." She said, leading us into the building. My first day as a Junior Wildlife Ranger had officially started.

14: The Wildlife Building

"The Wildlife Building is a modern, cutting-edge wildlife facility." Ms. Greene continued. "It was completed 3 years ago at a total cost of 1.5 million dollars, and every employee and volunteer here are very proud to be a part of it. It was paid for by funds from the Melburn Foundation, an environmental foundation that gives money to deserving wildlife organizations. The State of Florida also contributed to the costs and this is the magnificent result." She walked us to a room that was more quiet where we could sit down, then continued.

"I'd like to take this time to tell you a story about how the Melburn foundation became involved in this project. It all started when the Manager of this park, Bart Kane, met the director of the Melburn foundation, Ellie Miller. She called him to help her catch a hurt, stray dog that she wanted to help, but could not catch. At the time, Mr. Kane had no idea who she was, or that she was very rich, and he could have cared less. What he did care about was helping her catch that hurt and scared dog. After a few days he was successful, he safely caught the dog. He and Ellie took it to a Veterinarian to get it the help it needed, and the dog became Ellie's constant companion, she loved that dog very much! That is how the friendship between the Homosassa Wildlife Park and the Melburn foundation began. Who knew that one compassionate and selfless act could bring so much wealth and good fortune to our beloved wildlife park? Let's move on, everyone follow me to our next destination, the wildlife kitchen."

We followed her past some offices for the Wildlife Staff, including Ms.Greene's office. We ended up in a large rectangular room where several people were making diets for the animals.

"This is the kitchen, the hub of the building. You'll notice the diets of the animals are listed on the large eraser boards covering the walls above the sinks and counters. Over there are the walk-in freezers, refrigerators, and a large storage room for the dry goods. Across the room are bins for various types of dry feed, and then there's this; in these large rectangular bus tubs are some delicious meal worms!" Ms. Greene kidded us about the delicious part, but the worms were very real.

"What eats mealworms here, Ms. Greene?" A girl I hadn't met yet inquired. She was slender and tall, her posture perfect. Her hair was styled in box braids adorned with tiny gold stars and moons here and there around the braids. They complimented her flawless black skin. The words *chic* and edgy came to my mind when observing her style. I was instantly drawn to her.

"Mostly birds, Josephine, but some turtles love them too. I'm glad you asked. Mealworms provide protein for them. I need to show you all something else, come over here with me please."

She took us over to one of the walk-in refrigerators and opened the door. She walked in and it was so large we could all follow her in. Two sides of the walk-in were lined with industrial looking shelving units. Ms. Greene grabbed another bin, this one with a lid.

"Before I open this I need you to know that some animal diets consist of- how should I say this??? *Unpleasant* food. We feed them what they would eat in their natural environment. You have to accept that since you will be responsible for making their diets and feeding them."

With that she opened the lid, and low and behold it was filled with dead mice and rats. Before we could all digest that, she grabbed another bin and lifted the lid. That bin had dead baby chicks. I almost felt sick to my stomach, I wasn't quite sure I'd be able to eat lunch after seeing that.

"This is what Birds of Prey and snakes eat, it's just a fact of life. We make sure, however, to be as humane as we can be when sacrificing the life of an animal for an animal. It's all about respect and honor, really." Ms. Greene put the bin away and turned to us. "Working with wildlife is not very glamorous, is it? Let's move on, you'll have plenty of time later to get acquainted with making diets as it's one of your major responsibilities as a Wildlife Ranger."

We followed her to the next room.

"This is the employee break room, and there is also a laundry room, bathroom with showers, and beyond that is the Education room where we will be spending our time as Junior Rangers."

We continued to the far right of the building where we came upon two large doors with a sign that said, "**Medical Facilities.**" She pushed a button on the door to open it.

"This is our Wildlife Hospital and Rehabilitation Center. We have all the equipment you need to properly take care of the animals, such as x-ray machines, scales, ultrasound, and anesthesia machines. I am a Veterinarian as well as the Wildlife Supervisor, I am responsible for the health and well being of every animal residing here."

She continued past the hospital and opened another set of double doors.

"This area is the living quarters for the interns coming to our park to study and work with the wildlife here. The two current interns are standing right here, as they will be participating in our Academy. Drew and Serafina, why don't you give us a tour of your rooms?"

"I'd be happy to, Ms.Greene." Drew replied. "My room is to the left. Please excuse my mess."

He opened the door and we saw a nice room with a bunk bed, dresser, desk and a chair. "This room is very comfortable. I'm very happy I have the opportunity to stay here."

Serafina spoke up. "My room is down this hall on the left and it's an exact replica as Drew's only cleaner!" She laughed. "We also have a unisex bathroom with a shower over there." She pointed to it.

"Thanks Drew and Serafina for the tour." Ms.Greene said. "The final area to view in the building before we end up in the Education room is located at the back of the building, it is called the Quarantine area. It's a highly restricted area with limited access. When a new animal comes to the park it is first quarantined here for 30 days to determine it is healthy and has no communicable diseases before they are moved to an exhibit with other animals. It is also the area where we house Florida Black Bear cubs that have come to the park for unfortunate reasons, such as the mother being killed by a car. They are cared for until they can be reintroduced back to the wild when they are old enough. We have a strict 'No hands on' policy with the cubs, we limit human interaction as much as possible. We want them to stay wild, and not interact or depend on humans. The wildlife park has successfully released many bears back into the wild, something we are very proud of."

She led us to two more large doors labeled with the words:

Quarantine Area: RESTRICTED

"Please keep very quiet while back here, and keep a distance from the holding pens." She spoke in a whispered tone.

We followed her silently through the double doors and looked around. The quarantine area was situated outside but was completely sheltered with a roof and all the pens were made of concrete and had water pools. I counted 10 holding pens, all very large. Some were covered with large black tarps for privacy.

"Only the most trusted and experienced employees and volunteers are allowed to work back here. Any questions?" Ms.Greene asked us.

I raised my hand and she acknowledged me.

"How do you feed the bear cubs?" I quietly asked to be mindful of her request.

"If the cubs are very young we hand feed them a special milk formula for bears, but we do not cuddle or coo over them. If they are older, we feed them food they would actually eat in their natural habitat, such as nuts and berries. They also have to forage for their food, which just means we make them look and work for it. The pens are divided in two and there are gates that can be opened and closed. While the cubs are on one side of the pen, our staff will enter the other side and place their food. The rule is no contact. If the cubs become dependent on humans, it could be detrimental to their eventual release."

Another kid raised his hand that I didn't know.

"Ms.Greene, where are they released?" He asked her.

"They are usually released as close to the area they were originally found, as far away from human populations as possible. That is determined by the Florida Fish and Wildlife Conservation Commission, the agency responsible for bringing us the abandoned cubs in the first place."

We walked out of the quarantine area as quietly as we came in. Ms.Greene led us to our final destination, the Education room.

"Rangers, this is your area. These lockers are for your personal belongings. You will study here at this conference table. You report here at 7:00 a.m. sharp. This concludes your tour, I hope you have enjoyed it. Please get comfortable and take a seat at the table. Our next step is to get acquainted with each other. We are a team, as such we must know and trust one another."

We sat down and my Aunt Beth walked in. Ms.Greene introduced her.

"Rangers, this is Beth Kane, she is your Wildlife Ranger Leader, and the Education Director here at the park. She will take it from here, I will see you later. Goodbye for now." Our attention turned to my aunt, standing at the head of the table. It was time to get to know each other.

15: Getting Acquainted

"Hello Rangers! As Ms.Greene stated my name is Beth Kane. I have a degree in Environmental Education and have worked with animals for the past 20 years. I am married to Bart Kane, the Manager of this wonderful park. I have a son named Aiden, and my niece, Rayne Lancaster now lives with us for which I am very grateful." She glanced my way, putting her hand to her heart. "I'd like for us all to get to know each other, so let's start with each one of you taking a turn telling us about yourself. Who would like to go first?"

Maverick stood up. "I'll go, and then we can go on down the table." He suggested. "My name is Maverick Greene, I'm 15 years old, and I want to study Marine Biology or Zoology. I also love Baseball, I play the position shortstop on my high school team. Another passion of mine is kayaking on the Homosassa River, I go any chance I get. You just met my mother, Ms. Greene, the Wildlife Supervisor, and this girl sitting right here next to me is my pesky but lovable twin sister, Mallory. Your turn, sis." He sat down.

"Thanks Bro! Yes, we are twins, but obviously I am the better looking twin." We all laughed. "I want to be a Veterinarian like my mom, I also love kayaking and paddle boarding and Manatees. I'm so excited to be part of the Wildlife Academy, Maverick and I could not attend last summer because we had to stay with our dad in South Florida." Mallory finished. I was next in line so I stood up.

"My name is Rayne Lanecastor. I am 15 years old and I was born and raised in Cleveland, Ohio. I just moved here to Florida to live with my Uncle Bart, cousin Aiden, and Aunt Beth as she already mentioned. I'm not quite sure what my future holds but I do know it involves wildlife and the environment and I feel very fortunate and lucky to be here to learn what I can."

I kept it short and simple. Next was Jenzy.

"Hi! I'm Jenzy Jackson! I was born in Orlando Florida, but I love living in Homosassa. My dad is the Assistant Park Manager here at this park and my mom is a Librarian. I love manatees but I am really excited to learn about Florida reptiles! I think they are so underrated." Jenzy sat down and Drew McArthur took up where she left off.

"I am Drew McArthur, I'm 17 and my homeland is South Africa. I am here to study manatees, last year I studied lemurs on the island of Madagascar. I want to get a degree in Environmental Law, so I can help in the conservation of Wildlife. I'm excited to say I have been accepted into the University Of Miami next semester. I saw online the chance to intern here with Manatees and I convinced my parents to fund it. Fortunately they are very supportive. I am very appreciative that Ms. Greene agreed to be my chaperone for two months." He looked at Serafina and said, "Your turn, sunshine."

Serafina smiled at him as she gracefully stood up, placing one hand upon her hip. She reeked of confidence, she was drop dead gorgeous and she knew it. I decided I could learn a thing or two from her just by being in her presence.

"Hola a todos! I am Serafina Serrano, I am 17, and I am a Cuban Latino. I was born and raised in sunny & tropical Miami Beach in South Florida, otherwise known as SOFLO. I grew up living near the beach, I feel my best when I'm near the warm saltwater of the Atlantic Ocean. My favorite animal is the sea turtle, every March the female sea turtles start coming on shore to dig their nests and lay their eggs. A couple of months later the baby turtles hatch out of their eggs, digging their way out of their nests to begin their journeys to the sea. I spent countless hours as a child trying to help some get to the water, because some babies would get confused and go the wrong way!" She giggled. "As you are already aware I am also interning this summer at the park, with Ms.Greene chaperoning me." With that statement Serafina sat down as gracefully as she stood.

Sea turtles! How interesting she is, I thought. Two more to go. The girl named Josephine introduced herself. She was the complete opposite of Serafina in looks and attitude, making me instantly like her twice as much. I definitely wanted to get to know her better.

"I'm Josephine Adams and I'm 14. Please call me Josie. If you haven't noticed by now take a look at my left hand and you will see I have what some might call a handicap, but I call a blessing in disguise. I was born prematurely and was diagnosed with Cerebral palsy. I have no motor function in my hand, essentially it is paralyzed. Don't feel sorry for me, what you can do with two good hands I can do better with just one! I love all animals, being here is a dream come true." She radiated positive vibes, it was very appealing. I hadn't noticed her disability and I admired her spunk for just laying it all out on the table like that. I seriously loved her 'anything you can do, I can do better!' attitude. I looked at the end of the table to see the final Jr. ranger stand to introduce himself as Liam Morse, just turned 16. He told us his aspiration was to become employed as a wildlife ranger at the park and felt this would be a natural stepping stone on the path to get there. When he finished talking my Aunt Beth gave us all our own dark green t-shirts that had 'Jr. Wildlife Ranger' embroidered on the top left side of the shirt, as well as our own name tags to wear with it. To top it all off, we got these cool olive green Indiana Jones type of hats that said FLORIDA PARK SERVICE on them. Just when I thought the day couldn't get better, it did. Two volunteers walked in with multiple pizza boxes in their arms. Pizza is a universal conversation starter for sure, a staple for social gatherings. We spent the rest of the afternoon eating pizza and getting to know each other more. The day went quickly, and before I knew it, my first day as a Junior Wildlife Ranger ended. I loved every minute of it.

16: The Wildlife Park

Uncle Bart picked me up on the golf cart promptly at 2:00 p.m. after the academy ended to give me a personal tour of the wildlife park. The first stop was at the Reptile House which was actually pretty interesting. I wondered if I would ever be responsible for feeding any of the snakes--yuck. I could handle feeding the turtles no problem. Snakes, not so sure. Uncle Bart told me I would never go near the venomous snakes on exhibit, only the reptile experts have contact with them. Really good to hear. Next we drove through the first half of the "Wildlife Walk" area with multiple bird and mammal exhibits connected to a free flight Aviary. The Wildlife Walk & Aviary had several wildlife habitats joined together by wooden boardwalks and small bridges over a small, sparkling river. Some habitats were at eye level, some you looked down upon. The first thought that came to my mind seeing this area was "Enchanted Forest of Florida." It was magical, so much so you half expected to see Sleeping Beauty or Snow White living there, only they aren't, but some wonderful wildlife are! No matter where you looked there were birds and ducks of all shapes and sizes flying around freely amongst the lush green grass framed by native plants and trees. The diamond glint shimmer of water cascaded down from small man-made waterfalls leading to the small river, so pretty, so peaceful. One of my favorite bird exhibits that Uncle Bart showed me was the Whooping

Crane exhibit, not only because the cranes are so rare (they are very endangered) but because they are so regal and graceful. I actually knew a little about Whooping Cranes already, such as they were on the brink of extinction and there was a huge effort to save their species, and that once a year a group of Whooping Cranes follow an ultra light airplane all the way to Florida during migration.

"This is one area you will be working at, Rayne." My uncle said. "You will learn about Romeo and Juliet's story soon enough. That's the nicknames the two cranes were given from our staff. Their real names are Peepers and Levi. They have a rare and interesting love story." He chuckled. "Let's keep going for now."

The golf cart whisked us to the second half of the Wildlife Walk area to the land mammals exhibits. We drove by large habitat areas for Black Bears, Florida Panthers, Red Wolves, White-tailed deers and Key Deer, then stopped at Lu the Hippo's habitat.

"I stopped here Rayne, to introduce you to Lu, an African Hippopotamus. He has lived here since 1964 and is our most famous resident. He was born at the San Diego Zoo on January 26, 1960. During his early years he was featured in movies and television as a star with the Ivan Tors Animal Actors troupe, which wintered at the park while in private ownership. When the State of Florida acquired the park in 1989 it decided to focus on just native Florida wildlife and find other homes for all the exotic animals, Lu included. A public outcry ensued. That's when the local newspaper, the Citrus County Chronicle, reported the story which resulted in thousands of people partitioning the then Governor of Florida, Lawton Chiles, to keep Lu as a permanent resident of the park. Governor Chiles actually flew here to the park in 1991, personally granting Lu with a special Florida citizenship. Lu is now an honorary native Floridian. That is probably my favorite story about this park?"

I loved that story, too. I asked my uncle what Lu ate.

"He's a herbivore, so he eats Alfalfa Hay, watermelons, cantaloupe, apples, and herbivore pellets."

Lu saw my uncle and gave a loud greeting, *HUH HUH HUH HUH HUH HUUUUUT!!!*

I laughed out loud with delight. "It seems like he's talking to you, Uncle Bart! Does he recognize you?"

"Yes, he's very smart. You know, Hippopotamuses are considered to be the most dangerous animal in Africa, they are extremely aggressive and unpredictable. They kill more people than Lions and Crocodiles. Hard to believe when you look at Lu, right? You will learn to make diets for Lu, but that's the extent of your interaction with him. Only the most experienced Wildlife Rangers work with him, and no one is allowed to get in the water with him, or stand close to him, for obvious safety reasons. Let's move on to our final destination, I'm going to take you to the Underwater Observatory, also known as the Fishbowl?"

"This is so much fun, Uncle Bart! Thank you!" I jumped on the golf cart. We passed by the River Otter exhibits and the Alligator Habitat, ending up at a building called **"THE MOO."**

MOO stands for Manatee Operation Office." My uncle explained. "This is the place where the Rangers do all things associated with the manatees, record keeping, office work, diets. It has a changing room where we hang the dive suits and water shoes as well as a bathroom with a shower. You will be spending many hours here as part of your training."

We left the golf cart so we could walk a path that led us to the mouth of the Blue Springs. A short bridge took us to the Fishbowl, a small building on top of a huge circular underwater observatory. From there we climbed down some stairs leading to an underwater room. When we got to the bottom I was stunned by the spectacular 360 degree underwater view.

"These windows are made of 7 layers of plexiglass, they can handle the pressure of the water. Three times a week certified divers who volunteer here clean them on the outside. It's a great view of under the water, isn't it?" Uncle Bart asked me.

"It's unlike anything I've ever seen!" I replied in awe. Everywhere I looked I saw schools of fish, none of which I had ever seen before. There was also the manatees, and one was looking directly at us while munching on something green and leafy looking. There were areas of rock formations marked with caverns and pathways, like an underwater maze.

A large group of fish slowly meandered in front of us, they were long and silver and sleek with a thin black line running down their sides.

"What kind of fish are they?" I asked.

"Those are Snook fish, Rayne, and a favorite of fishermen to catch, as they are fun to catch and delicious too. You can only fish for them in their season, though, they are protected."

Oh! The Snook fish my Aunt previously talked about, I recalled.

Each panel of glass exposed something wonderful and different. My uncle pointed out groups of all kinds of fish, Sheepshead, Redfish, Tarpon, and Mangrove Snappers. No wonder this underwater observatory is nick-named the fishbowl! As we gazed at the fish another manatee popped up into our view, stopping to stare at us as we stared at it.

"That's Betsy, she's been here at the park for 30 years. Unfortunately she was permanently injured by a boat strike. She has three long scars on the top right side of her body from the boats propellers. She has tons of personality!" My uncle said.

"She's incredible, Uncle Bart!" I replied. "Will I get to work with her?"

"Yes, Rayne, you will."

"I love it, love the park. You must be so proud to be the Manager here. I've never seen such a pretty paradise, with such interesting wild-life. I miss my mom so much, but I know that she's smiling down on me from heaven, I can just feel her all around me." Thinking of my mom, I stopped talking for a minute because I felt myself starting to tremble with the slightest surge of sadness. So cruel, that sadness! Just then my gaze fell upon Betsy's sweet face. Two bright black button eyes bore into mine, and the sadness I felt suddenly slipped away. I couldn't be unhappy while looking upon such beauty and pure goodness.

"Thank you for the tour." I added.

"You're welcome, Rayne. It looks like it's about to storm, so let's go home and see what my lovely wife has made for dinner. She knew it would be a long day for you, and I'm starved!"

We got back in the cart and headed back to the house. My home now. Wow. I closed my eyes and silently thanked my mom. We got there just before the rain started, and boy when it started it came down with thunder and lightning that was quite furious! This must be one of the afternoon storm showers I read about. I ran inside with my Uncle Bart then ate another delicious meal made by Aunt Beth. By the time we finished dinner the storm had finished too, it left as fast as it came. Story of my life, I thought, one minute sunny and bright, the next stormy and dark. #outofdarknesscomeslight

17: Pelican Rehabilitation

After helping clean the dinner dishes I decided to go check on the pelican that Maverick had rescued that first day I met him. I wondered how the pelican was doing, and a walk would feel good after I had totally pigged out. I asked Aiden if he wanted to go with me, he enthusiastically said yes. I grew up a single child, I never knew what I was missing not having a sibling until now. Aiden is just a joy to be around, so cute, smart too. I wanted him to hopefully love me as a sister one day, as I loved him like a little brother now. Another blessing, I thought. My Uncle Bart let me know that there was a Wildlife Ranger named Sheri on duty at the hospital working the late shift. As we walked Aiden talked about living at the Wildlife Park.

"I know I'm lucky, Rayne, not many kids can say they live at a wildlife nature park. All my friends think I'm lucky too. What's Ohio like? Do you miss it?"

"Ohio is beautiful like Florida, just vastly different. You have some big cities, and you have the rural farm areas, land stretching untouched for miles. It gets very cold in the winter, and it snows for months on end. Snow is great at first, but you get tired of it after awhile. Like when it turns brown, or icy, or when it snows so much you have to dig your way out of your house. Not so great then. On the plus side, the people of Ohio are friendly and there are two very nice Zoo and Aquariums, one in my hometown of Cleveland and another one in Cincinnati. The Ohio wildlife consists of White-tailed deer, opossums, squirrels, and raccoons. Yes, I miss it even though it hasn't been that long. I suppose I will always miss it, but I've closed that particular chapter of my life. Can you understand that, Aiden?"

"I get it. You've started a new chapter in your life here in Florida, right?" He grinned adorably at me.

"Exactly!" I answered, grinning back. "With a new family, too. Lucky me!" I put my arm around his shoulder. "Look, we're here! I sure hope Mrs. Pelican is O.K!"

We walked inside and turned the corner leading to the employee break room. I stopped short then, because what I saw made me instantly wish I wasn't there. Maverick and Serafina were sitting close together deep in conversation. I felt like I was intruding. **#Awkward!** She was smiling at him adoringly as he talked to her. I knew right then and there that she liked him more than just as a friend. She has good taste, I miserably acknowledged. Aiden saw Maverick (thankfully ending my awkward silence) greeting him with a "Hey Maverick! Rayne and I are here to see the pelican you saved!"

"Is that so, buddy?" He stood up and gave Aiden a fist bump. "Well it happens to be time to feed her dinner, so you two can assist me with that."

"Are you sure?" I asked, looking over at Serafina who wasn't looking very pleased at the moment. "We don't want to interrupt you if you are busy."

"You're not interrupting. I was just talking with Serafina about an orphaned otter pup on its way here. We had to discuss it's diet, what habitat has to be set up, and the importance of safety protocol caring for it. Otter babies are cute, but have sharp teeth. I'll teach you how to work with and take care of it too, if you'd like."

I was almost able to ignore and forget that Serafina was glaring straight at me with a frown upon her pouting lips. I did but I knew *she* wouldn't and I was surprisingly ok with that.

"Yes, I'd like that very much Maverick. Hello Serafina, how are you?" I looked at her. I wanted to try to be friends with her. She looked at me and seemed to force her lips into a smile.

"I'm fine, thank you, I was just enjoying the most interesting conversation with the most *interesting* guy." She touched Mavericks arm, giving him a dazzling smile. Maverick turned away from her shaking his head with a quizzical half smile.

"I guess animal husbandry is interesting, at least to all of us. See you later, Serafina. Aiden and Rayne, follow me."

We followed him but when I looked back at Serafina her arms were crossed over her chest and she looked very displeased. ***#UhOh!***

We went to the kitchen. Sheri the Wildlife Ranger was there making diets.

"Here you go, Maverick." She handed him a bowl filled with silver fish laying on ice. "I'm giving her 10 fish, her appetite has been increasing. She is getting stronger everyday. You'll be able to release her back to the environment soon." Sheri gave him the good news. She greeted Aiden and he introduced us.

"Very nice to meet you, Rayne." Her smile was wide and infectious, the kind that made you smile back just as widely as hers. Her black hair was placed in a perfectly messy bun on the top of her head, a few stray tendrils managed to escape and now framed her face, prettily so. She was welcoming and warm just like a Rainbow after a Rain shower. I said it was nice to meet her too then we all walked out to the hospital recovery pens located outside. Mrs. Pelican was in pen number 4. When she saw Maverick holding her dinner she started flapping her wings and snapping her beak open and closed. Sheri asked Aiden and I to stand to the side then she opened the gated door to Mrs. Pelicans pen. Maverick winked at me then went inside.

"Watch what happens when I throw her a fish, you'll see her throat pouch expand and you'll be able to see the many stitches she got sewing up the hole she had. There you go, Darlin!" He said to Mrs. Pelican, NOT me. Mrs. Pelican very quickly ate the fish like a champ. Maverick and Sheri looked over her wound and declared it to be healing perfectly well. Maverick showed us Mrs. Pelican's information chart, writing down his observations and recording her diet intake.

"We keep detailed records of every patient who comes to the hospital, it's a very important part of working with animals." Maverick explained.

"Mrs. Pelican seems to be doing very well, that's so great!" I happily exclaimed. "Good for you saving her, Maverick, I'm so impressed!"

"Is that what you call her, Rayne? Mrs. Pelican?" He chuckled, amused.

"Yes, it is. Is that funny?"

"No, it's appropriate. I'm glad you're impressed, big time. Thanks." He looked at me with a stare that gave me goosebumps.

"You're welcome, Maverick." I could stare at his cute face forever and never get tired of looking at it, I realized. *#UhOhAgain!* Remembering how adoringly Serafina was looking at him earlier made me realize something else. I was going to have to stand in line. Big bummer, HUGE.

Aiden and I said our goodbye's then headed home. Our visit to the Wildlife Hospital was the perfect end to a perfect day.

18: Wildlife Ranger Safety Guidelines

Personal Safety

1. Be prepared physically and mentally for the workday. Regular sleep and a good diet helps you to stay focused.

2. Maintain a positive attitude. Animals tend to be sensitive to their environment, keeper activity, and associated moods.

3. Be careful when using over the counter medications. A large number of Antihistamines tend to cause drowsiness. If taking prescription medications, be aware of side-effects and drug interaction warnings.

4. Dress appropriately for different weather conditions and for the specific tasks that are required in your work area. Gloves and good footwear are always second thoughts until the need for repairs, running, or climbing occurs.

5. Make sure you have the proper tools available for your specific work area, and that they are in good working order.

6. tay hydrated! The Florida heat can be brutally hot, and if you do not drink water constantly you might become in danger

of suffering from heatstroke. Drink water before, during, and after your shifts.

Animal Safety

1. Know the medical history, personal history, and personalities of the wildlife in your care. This includes a working knowledge of the established Hierarchies in family groups, colonies, and herds.

2. Always read the daily report for your section or work area. This is the best way to find out what is happening on a daily basis with the animals, projects, and staff.

3. Monitor the animals continually for any changes in behavior. A change in established behaviors could be due to environmental stress or physical problems. If the animal seems stressed, extra care should be taken.

4. Always know where your animals are. This applies especially to shift procedures for potentially dangerous animals.

5. Be aware of zoonotic diseases. Use gloves and masks when necessary, and always wash hands and disinfect equipment regularly.

Exhibit Safety

1. Always lock security chains, gates, and doors that control access to to keeper work areas. This should be done every time someone enters or leaves an area. This keeps the public out and provides another layer of animal containment.

2. Check locks on exhibits before leaving an area, and check locks when returning to an area. Inspect locks, shift doors, pulleys and ropes on a regular basis. Periodic preventative maintenance can catch most mechanical problems before they become safety concerns.

3. Inspect exhibits/habitats on a daily basis.

4. Double-check everything and assume nothing. If something in the exhibit/habitat area looks unsafe, stop, step back, and take a second look. There is nothing wrong with relying on your intuition if something doesn't "feel right."

5. Double-check every lock on every exhibit. You can never go wrong with checking a lock twice.

I stared at the Wildlife Ranger's safety guidelines thinking about the first week of the Wildlife Ranger Academy. We spent most of the time learning about cleaning habitats and safety procedures as well as ranger work duties. We also learned how to make the diets of every animal at the park. I liked making diets because it provided me time to spend with my fellow rangers, to get to know them better. I spent Friday morning with Josephine doing just that. We thawed out fish, baby chicks and mice. We sprinkled many diets with mealworms or crickets. Quality bonding time. We both decided that this was definitely NOT a glamorous part of the job.

"I'm a little bit grossed out, Josephine." I admitted.

"Yep. It's definitely gross." She concurred. "And please, call me Josie. All my friends do."

The loss of ability to use her left hand was barely noticeable, she was so agile and strong with her right hand. She made diets faster than I did, including the ones that needed varying sizes of cut up fruits and vegetables. Naturally she finished her diets first. She sat upon the table next to me and started up a very serious conversation.

"I heard you lost both your parents and that you just moved here to Florida to live with your aunt and uncle. Is that true?" She asked.

"Well, yes, it is, except I didn't 'lose' my parents they both died."

"I'm sorry about your parents, I hope you don't mind me being so upfront and direct. I'd like to genuinely get to know you better."

"It's all good. Don't be sorry. upfront and direct is good by me. Ask me anything."

So she did. "Have you ever shared a real kiss with anyone?"

My answer; "No."

"Would you like to travel the world?"

"Yes, absolutely!"

"What do like to do for fun?"

"Read. Use my iPad for knowledge. Write."

"Do you ever get sad?"

"I 'lost' both my parents. So, that's a yes.

She smiled a little. I was relieved she got my dark humor. She continued.

"Do you believe in God?"

"Yes."

"Why?"

"Because I believe in love. Wherever you see or have love, there is God. Timeless love. Infinite love. Endless love. My turn to ask questions. Is that cool with you?"

"Go for it." She affirmed.

"Have *you* ever shared a kiss with someone?" I asked.

"My answer to that is unfortunately yes. It sucked. It was with my next door neighbor. It was sloppy and wet. He actually tried to stick his tongue in my mouth, yuck! Killed any kisses for me again in the near future..."

"Very sorry to hear that, Josie. Next question; what makes you happy?"

"Animals, Japanese Anime, the beach, running as exercise, it's like meditation for me."

"What makes you sad?"

"Animal cruelty, racism, bigotry, mean spirited people, fake people."

"What do you want to be when you grow up?"

She stayed silent for a moment deep in thought, then answered.

"I want to travel the world, be CEO of my own company, be an animal advocate, marry my soulmate and have 2 children!"

"Sounds like a great future, Josie. It's really nice getting to know you."

I finished my last diet and we cleaned up our work stations. I invited her to the sleepover but she had other plans for the weekend.

"Thanks for the invite though, maybe next time. I enjoyed getting to know you too, Rayne, I can tell you're a Girl's Girl. You're down to earth and you have a great sense of humor."

"I think the same about you, Josie."

The rest of the day went by quickly. My first week at the Wildlife Academy was now officially over and I was excited for the weekend, especially for the sleepover Saturday night. I was thrilled to have new friends that I liked so much. My new life in Florida was going good. *Really* good. **#grateful**

19: A Saturday Surprise

I woke up Saturday morning refreshed and full of energy. My Aunt Beth invited me to a breakfast of coffee (her) and green tea with honey (me) and croissants on the porch. When I walked outside to the porch I was greeted with a warm wave of heat. You know the kind of heat that you feel when you're in the bathroom after a hot shower? It was that kind of heat. Thankfully the shade of the porch made the heat tolerable. I took a seat next to my aunt.

"How did you like your first week of the Academy, Rayne?"

"I loved it. I can't wait to learn all the information I can concerning animals."

We planned the slumber party and she offered to take me to the grocery store for supplies. We just finished eating our breakfast when I got an unexpected and heart palpitating surprise. My aunt saw him before I did.

"We have a visitor, Rayne. It's Maverick Greene. I wonder what he wants..?"

"Good morning, Mrs. Kane, hello Rayne." Maverick greeted us. His hair was tied back, casually, perfectly so. It complimented his insanely perfect jawline.

"It's a gorgeous morning isn't it, Maverick?" My aunt asked.

"It sure is, Mrs. Kane, the humidity is not too bad and there is a nice cool wind on the water. That's why I'm here. I'm going Kayaking, I thought I'd ask Rayne if she wanted to join me, if that's alright with you?"

"Of course it is, Maverick. Would you like to go, Rayne?" She asked me.

"I would like that very much, Maverick! Thank you! Give me a minute to change and get my water shoes."

I left the two of them on the porch to talk while I ran upstairs to my room. I put my hair up high into a ponytail and added some lip gloss to my lips. I was now ready to kayak. With Maverick. Again I had 'Butterflies' in my stomach. Seemed like it was happening to me continuously lately. I said goodbye to my Aunt Beth and walked with Maverick down the pathway to the dock I had visited before with Aiden.

We were halfway to the dock when a break in the trees exposed a huge ray of sunlight causing me to pause for a minute. I tilted my face upward to feel the pleasantly warm sun on my face. Being in Nature like this was my utopia. As I was soaking up the sun, I felt another unusual sensation, I intuitively felt Mavericks eyes looking at me, even though I wasn't looking at him! I turned around to look and see. When I did, my eyes locked on to his. He *was* looking at me, after all.

"Don't move." He asked/said. I stood still. In that moment I couldn't move if I wanted to. He reached over me to capture my ponytail in his hands. He held it up gently to the sun. "Your hair really does resemble the color of rose gold, shimmering in the sun." He murmured softly.

"Ummmm, uh, oh, ok., thanks." Apparently I had lost the ability to form a coherent sentence. I know I blushed, I felt it. He let go of my hair and we walked on. I spent the rest of the walk to the dock just trying to calm down my now fast beating heart.

We reached the dock and I saw that Maverick brought a bright yellow, double kayak and a slim life vest for me. He explained that I should always wear it even when I became adept at kayaking by myself. Better to be prepared and safe than sorry. He helped me sit down at the back of the kayak and I got comfortable. He handed me the paddles to hold while he joined me on the the kayak. When he was ready, I gave him his paddle and off we went.

"As you can see the paddle is flat on both ends so you can paddle on both sides without having to physically switch it from one side to the other. Hold the paddle with both hands placed in the middle, palms down. Just relax and get into a rhythm of right left, right left, right left. When you get tired of paddling just rest the paddle on your knees and glide for a while. I sat in the front this time so you could watch my movements. Next time you can sit in the front and I'll take the back. I think I'd enjoy the view much better that way..." His voice trailed off and I wondered what he meant by that comment. A better view, as in looking at me? I know my view of Maverick paddling the kayak with strong, muscular arms was indeed an awesome view. Maverick told me he was taking me on a tour of the Homosassa river and springs and to all the spots he knew where we could see some wildlife. After about 30 minutes of paddling we passed by the wildlife park's Blue Springs area, multiple houses situated on the water, a couple of waterfront restaurants, and one very charming and quaint fish house.

"That's where the locals here buy their fresh fish and shrimp to eat, the fishermen and shrimpers all sell some of their days catch there."

"I tried Grouper recently, it was delicious!" I told him. After a few minutes Maverick spoke again.

"I'm taking you to a special place, called Shell Island. It's a privately owned small island that has a vacation home on it called 'The Treehouse.' Only one person lives there year round, the Treehouse Caretaker, who happens to be a family friend. We're close to it now, it will give us a chance to stretch our legs for a bit. I also have a small surprise for you there."

A surprise! I was extremely flattered. **#awesomesauce!**

"Thank you, Maverick, this is a wonderful adventure! I'm enjoying every minute of it."

A few minutes later we reached our destination.

"There she is, Rayne, Shell Island. Cool, right?"

"Very." I said to him. What happened next was even cooler. Much to my delighted surprise, a pod of dolphins swam by us playfully, swiftly bobbing up and down in the crystal clear water. "Look Maverick, dolphins!"

Maverick stopped paddling so we could observe them.

I couldn't contain my laughter watching them play, jumping out of the water and twirling around like graceful ballerina's. As much as we were watching them, they were watching us. They would take turns coming up alongside the kayak to intently stare at us, even the baby. They were long and silvery sleek, with intelligent eyes looking back at us with keen observation. I counted 5 in total, and one was clearly smaller than the rest. A family. I couldn't believe I was seeing them so close in their natural environment. I couldn't tear my gaze away from them, I was completely enthralled by what I was witnessing. We stayed like that until they swam away.

"I love dolphins." Maverick said. "They are magnificent creatures. When they look you in the eyes it's as if they can see your soul."

I wholeheartedly agreed. We glided up to the dock of Shell Island. Maverick got out first then extended his hand to me to help pull me up onto the dock. When I reached the top I spontaneously hugged him, I was filled with joy seeing the dolphins and I wanted to thank him.

"Thank you Maverick so much for bringing me here!" I put my arms up around his shoulders and squeezed him tight. He responded by hugging me back, with his arms wrapping behind my back. It was a quick hug but it felt really nice. Maverick smiled his killer smile and let me go.

"Your welcome, Rayne. I like seeing you smile. Let's go to the house and freshen up, then I'll show you your surprise."

The Treehouse was a large two story stilt home surrounded by tall trees. The house had large windows and was surrounded by a wraparound porch on the top level. You had to climb a wooden staircase to enter, it was exactly like what I imagined a treehouse would look like, only better, because it had a 360° view of the water. We were greeted by a man who can only be described as commanding. He reminded me of a Pirate, or maybe a Captain of a ship- a rough and tough man to be sure. His weathered sun bronzed skin was lined with wrinkles from constant exposure to the sun. He was bald, but had a full beard of unruly salt and pepper colored hair. I might have been intimidated by him until I saw his reaction to seeing Maverick.

"It's been a long time since I've seen you, boy!" His happy grin belied his imposing appearance, revealing the real man. He hugged Maverick just like I did moments before. Maverick introduced us.

"Rayne, meet Captain Dave. He is an icon in these parts, and he is the caretaker of the Island. He lives here full time." (So I was right, he was a Captain!)

"Nice to meet ya, young lady, and thanks for bringing this young scalawag here for a visit."

"Very nice to meet you too, Sir. I am happy to meet your acquaintance."

"You can just call me Captain, Rayne, I see you're just as good mannered as you are smart. Would you like a tour of the house?"

"I'd love it, Captain!"

The house was open, airy, and full of light. The large windows exposed a spectacular view of the turquoise Gulf waters. It had three bedrooms, two bathrooms, and an open concept kitchen/living room area. I'd love to own a place just like this one day, I thought. When the tour was done I excused myself to use the restroom. When I looked in the bathroom mirror I noticed my skin was turning rosy pink from the sun. I should have brought a hat, or sunscreen. Lesson learned for my next kayaking adventure, I murmured to myself. Overall I liked the effect the sun had on my skin, it was much better than my normally pale hue, a marked contrast from that sorrowful day when I looked in the mirror in the hospital bathroom. I joined Maverick in the kitchen.

"Ready for your surprise?" He asked me.

"Oh yes, definitely!" I answered.

He led me outside. A small white gravel path led to a picnic table shaded by a large green umbrella. The table had a large picnic basket on it. There was also a clear glass pitcher filled with ice and what appeared to be pink lemonade. Best surprise, EVER. Maverick had made us a picnic!

"A picnic for us, Maverick? I love it! You are so thoughtful!"

"I thought you might be hungry, I know I am. I called the Captain and arranged this earlier. He was happy to help. We've been close since I was a young and wild kid kayaking on the river. We met rescuing an injured manatee. It took us four days to rescue him. Nobody knows these waters better than the Captain." He started unpacking the basket of food so I filled our glasses with what was in the pitcher, which did indeed turn out to be some very tasty and thirst quenching pink lemonade. Maverick laid out a small platter of fruit and cheese, as well as two grilled cheese sandwiches. He also pulled out two slices of what looked to be homemade Key lime pie. We sat at the table and chowed down.

"Maverick, grilled cheese sandwiches are an American staple, they happen to be one of my favorite sandwiches." I said in between bites.

"That's something we have in common, Rayne. They're my favorite too."

I noticed there was a large fire pit area nearby surrounded by four long benches. There was also a large white hammock tied between two tall Palm trees. It was gently swaying in the wind. All of this overlooked the waters of the Gulf and Homosassa river. A person could never get tired of this view, I said to Maverick. He agreed and pointed to a large bird flying above us, which he called an Osprey. It had brown wings with a white feathered chest and head.

"The Osprey is also known as a Sea Hawk and is a Bird of Prey. That's its nest over there." Maverick pointed to a large nest high up in a tree. "Right now it's circling the water looking for a fish to eat."

"I hope it finds one and then we'll both be full."

We looked at each other and laughed. Maverick reached out to touch my cheek.

"You're getting slightly sunburned, Rayne. It suits you." He was looking at me with such intensity I found myself holding my breath. His fingers felt cool against my warm cheek, I found myself wanting him to kiss me, hoping he would. He didn't. I took a deep breath of fresh and pure Florida air as he dropped his hand. I could breathe again, I noticed. That's good. However, Maverick didn't kiss me, and that wasn't. Maybe he liked Serafina after all. I helped Maverick clean up and we went to the lodge to drop off our basket and utensils. We said our goodbyes to the Captain then kayaked away from a special place I could never forget.

"Here Rayne, put some of this on." Maverick handed me a bottle of sunblock he got from a very small compartment in the Kayak.

"O.k. Thanks, Mav." I rubbed some on my face, arms, and legs while he paddled.

"You called me Mav. I like that. It means your getting comfortable around me."

"I am. Your proving to be a good friend."

"Uh-Oh. Did I just get friend zoned?" He laughed.

I didn't tell him he was so out of the friend zone-WAY out. Definitely boyfriend material all the way.

"There aren't too many rules and regulations for kayaking. Two things are required though; one is having a life vest on the kayak, the second is to carry a small device that emits sound, like a whistle. So I have something for you." He paused his paddling for a minute then reached inside the small compartment again to take something else out.

Maverick handed me a bright silver whistle attached to a long silver chain. It gleamed brightly in the sun when I held it up.

"This is no ordinary whistle, it's a Marine whistle, and it's to be used to gain attention if you find yourself in distress." He turned to face me and slipped it around my neck. The contact of his hands moving my hair out of the way sent shivers down my spine.

"Now if you ever need me you can just whistle!" Maverick said. I thanked him and thought I'd be wearing AND using this whistle...A LOT.

We paddled back home and there was a few times where I had to rest and let him paddle by himself. He never seemed to get tired, but my arms sure did. Kayaking is a great workout, I concluded. As we were entering the Blue Water Springs area near the park we stopped to admire a group of manatees grazing for food. I saw a mother and calf which could have been the same mother and calf I met on the dock last weekend because I noticed the propeller marks/scars on the mothers side. I pointed her out Maverick, he was very familiar with her.

"Her name is Rose because she has a rose shaped scar pattern near her tail. Can you see it?" He pointed to it. I nodded yes and he continued. "She has lived in these waters for years now, this is the second calf that I know of that she has given birth to. She is one of my favorite manatees. She is very gentle and sweet."

It was a peaceful moment but only for a few minutes, because as we were observing the manatees a small, dull grey boat with bright orange stripes came speeding right toward us and the manatees- I was so afraid the boat would hit us or Rose and her baby! I noticed two men on the boat hooting and hollering, paying no intention whatsoever to what was in front of them. I heard Maverick swear something under his breath while paddling very swiftly and powerfully out of the way-succeeding just in the nick of time with my help.

"Brace yourself for the wake, Rayne, it's going to be big."

I held on tightly to the kayak as the waves came our way. We swelled up and down twice landing rather harshly each time but thankfully we didn't tip over.

"Curse those Hicks Brothers!" Maverick swore. He sounded *really* mad. I was just trying to stop trembling while looking to see if the manatees were hurt.

"Are you O.K., Rayne?" He turned his body to face me.

"I'm fine, thanks. Just a little shaken, that was scary. You know those men? Do all boats go that fast around here?"

"Yes, I know them Rayne, the whole family is bad news. Everyone in this area knows the Hicks family, they have been nothing but trouble for three generations. I swear they just get meaner all the time. They think that the normal rules of society do not apply to them. The Blue Water Springs area is protected by law to use idle speed here. Not that any of them care. The Hicks live in old Homosassa in a run down part of town. I don't see them on the water too much and that's a good thing."

"Well if I ever see their boat again I will avoid it at all costs!" I declared.

"Good idea." Maverick replied. "Another good idea is to kayak with someone else if you want to go further away from home, I go alone all the time but I'm very experienced, I've been kayaking on these waters for years."

We circled the area to see if the manatees were run over or injured by the speeding boat propellers. We didn't see anything out of the ordinary (thank goodness!) so we headed home. Maverick walked me to the front door. I thanked him for a wonderful afternoon.

"I had fun, Rayne, thanks for coming. Let's do it again soon."

"Deal!" I watched him walk away then I went to my room, collapsing on my bed. I passed out, taking a much needed nap. I probably would have slept all night if my aunt hadn't woke me up asking me if I would still like to go to the grocery store with her for the slumber party. The slumber party! I almost forgot about that! I met her downstairs and off we went.

20: Saturday Night Sleepover

At the grocery store I got the ingredients for making waffles (eggs, waffle mix, milk & a very good quality vanilla extract). I also bought heavy whipping cream and powdered sugar to make real whipped cream. I picked up strawberries, Sprite, Dr. Pepper, a couple of frozen pizza's and a huge bag of Doritos because who doesn't like Doritos? To finish it off I bought a bag of miniature bites caramel Milky Way bars for Jenzy and a bag of gummy bears for Mallory. I was going to have to eat healthy food all week to make up for a junk food filled weekend, but a slumber party without junk food just wasn't a party. After the grocery store my aunt insisted we go to the Krispy Kreme store to get some 'Hot off the Line' donuts. She pointed out the brightly lit **HOT NOW** red neon sign at the front of the store that meant you could get your donuts fresh that were just made. We walked in and bought 2 dozen donuts, one dozen glazed, the other raspberry jelly filled. When we got back into the car we each grabbed one to devour, there was no resisting. Again it was the most mind blowing, delicious donut I had ever eaten. Each bite literally melted in my mouth, inducing a sweet sugary sensation. I told my Aunt Beth that coming there was a brilliant idea, and it was. Maybe I'll own a Krispy Kreme store one day- not a bad thought. I knew one thing, my guests would be happy to see them. **#KrispyKremeFanForLifeAgain!** When we got home I mixed the whipped cream for the waffles I would make in the morning, then cleaned my 'lounge' to perfection. I still had an hour to go before Mallory and Jenzy came over so I got my iPad and turned it on. I searched the letters my mom had previously written for me, looking for just the right one to read. I wanted so badly to talk to her about all of the good things happening to me recently-Oh how I missed talking to her! I saw a letter titled: For the times when you miss me. It was perfect. I opened it up and started reading.

For the times when you miss me

Hello my darling daughter. Let me start off with I LOVE YOU VERY MUCH AND ALWAYS WILL! I know you miss me, so I want you to close your eyes and imagine me giving you a long hug accompanied by a kiss on your forehead. You also need to tell yourself a couple of things and know they are true:

1. *I am happy in Heaven with your father. We are your Guardian Angels now.*
2. *I do not want you to be sad. I want you to be happy.*
3. *Live every moment of your life as much as you can. Appreciate life.*
4. *I am so very proud of you!*
5. *We will be united together again someday, it will be a joyous occasion. Before that happens you have to live a very long and fulfilling life.*

I want you to read this note every time you start to feel sad and miss me.

I LOVE LOVE LOVE LOVE YOU! ALWAYS AND FOREVER! (Isn't this iPad great by the way?) LOVE ALWAYS- MOM

I loved these letters my mom wrote to me, I knew I'd treasure them forever. How thoughtful of her to write them for me. I had all these letters backed up on my computer so I would never be in danger of losing them. One day soon I would print them out and put them in a really special nice folder. I put my iPad away and went downstairs to spend time with my new family while I waited on my new friends.

Mallory and Jenzy arrived promptly at 6. We went upstairs and immediately began having fun. We were all hungry so I put the pizza's in the oven.

"I flippin love your space here, Rayne!" Mallory exclaimed. "After such a long week at the Academy I could use some chill time."

"Me too." Jenzy added. "It was an intense week. I'm glad we're doing this."

"Same." I agreed.

"Let's all get in our pajamas and get comfortable right now!" suggested Mallory. We changed then laid out blankets and pillows in the living room. We wolfed down the pizza, all the while talking about anything and everything. I brought out the donuts and candy I got for our slumber party, they both were thrilled I bought the junk food they loved.

"Rayyyyyyne I just love Gummy bears!" Mallory drawled. It's hilarious how she talks, extending some words. "Yummm." she added.

"Yes Rayne, thank you for having Dr. Pepper and caramel Milky Way bars. Pizza too! That was so thoughtful of you! Best sleepover *ever*!" Jenzy declared.

"The donuts were my aunts idea. I'm going to dig into them later on. My goodness those donuts are positively addicting!" I claimed.

"My brother told me you two went kayaking this morning. Did you have fun?" Mallory asked me.

"Yes I did, it was so nice of him to show me how to kayak properly and give me a tour of the Homosassa river and Gulf, he even took me to Shell Island."

"I think he's crushing on you Rayne. He's asked me so many questions about you. It's sooooo annoying." Mallory dramatically rolled her eyes.

I tried not to show my excitement about her saying Maverick was 'Crushing' on me. I played it cool but in my mind I was doing cartwheels.

"Me? Really? I thought he might like Serafina. I've seen them together a few times talking."

"Oh my goodness I sure hope not! Serafina is a mean girl... Jenzy and I don't care for her at all! She's so fake to me, pretending to be my friend just to get close to my brother." She rolled her eyes again.

"Maverick is oblivious to her obvious flirtation. Sometimes guys are so dense. I agree with Mallory, she is a mean girl." Jenzy said.

"She's very beautiful." I mused aloud.

"On the outside, sure." Jenzy responded. "On the inside, different story. She's cold, condescending and knows she will get what she wants, when she wants it. She has to be the center of attention, thrives on it. Here's an example of what I mean. Yesterday afternoon a reporter from the Chronicle came to the Wildlife Building to write a story about the baby otters we are rehabilitating. The reporter noticed I was bottle feeding one and began to ask me questions when Serafina intervened and hijacked the entire interview. I have to give her props for how smoothly she took over. She simply walked up to the reporter, smiled a dazzling smile, and said to him: 'I apologize but the otter must not be disturbed while being fed. I would be more than happy to answer your questions in the Education room.' Then she walked toward the Education room and he followed her there like a puppy dog. I don't care that she took over the interview, really I don't, but I just can't stand how she just has to 'rule the school' so to speak.

"How utterly rude!" Mallory said. "Also completely not surprising."

I told Jenzy I was sorry her interview was taken from her. I took the opportunity to ask Mallory about the look on her face that morning I met Drew and Serafina for the first time.

"Mallory, you looked like you were frowning when Serafina came into our view the first morning at the Wildlife building, as we were talking to Maverick and Drew. What was that about?"

Mallory paused a second before answering, obviously thinking carefully about what to say.

"I don't like or trust Serafina, every time she's around I feel uneasy, that's all really. Also, and I HATE to admit this, but I think I'm jealous of her. I really like Drew, and she's always so touchy feely with him, just like she is with my brother. It's irritating as heck."

Jenzy seemed amused by Mallory's almost cursing. She asked Mallory what she liked about Drew, besides his obvious good looks.

"Drew is the kind of guy that walks in a room and everyone there immediately wants to be near him. He's funny, engaging, the life of the party. He's larger than life! To top it off, he's so freaking cute, I can't stand it. He makes me laugh all the time, when I'm around him I feel all warm and fuzzy. Does that make sense?" She asked us.

"I get it." Jenzy told her. "He's a total snack-attack."

"I get it too." I said, and I really did. Because I felt exactly the same way about her brother. We spent the rest of the night laughing, eating more junk food, watching a movie, and dancing to our favorite music. When we thought we were tired we went to bed, but ended up talking almost all night long. It turned out to be one of the best nights with friends I've ever had.

21: Sunday Fun-day

We slept in the next morning waking up late in the afternoon ready to tackle the rest of the day. I made my famous waffles with fresh whipped cream, maple syrup and strawberries. Mallory made me laugh with all the *oohs* and *aaaahs* she kept moaning in between bites and Jenzy said they were the best she ever tasted. I asked what we were going to do today and Mallory came up with a great idea.

"Why don't we go paddle boarding?" She suggested.

"I'm in." Jenzy said.

"Me too. I'm psyched to learn how to paddle board." I concurred.

We changed in to our bathing suits then went down to the Garden of Springs where the kayaks and paddle boards were kept. There were two paddle boards and one kayak still available, so we signed them out and got started. Jenzy said she would take the kayak because Mallory is the best at paddle boarding, she could teach me better. The sun was out in full force, it was blazing. This time I was well prepared, I put on a ton of sun protection lotion and I wore a hat.

"Are you ready for your paddle board instruction, Rayne?" Mallory asked.

"Yes! Let's do this!" I was nervous, but determined.

We carried the large boards to the water, it felt so great getting in, so cool and refreshing it took the sting out of the sun's unrelenting rays.

"Most people who paddle board refer to it as 'SUP' which is abbreviated for stand up paddle boarding. Start by laying horizontal on your board, keeping your paddle blade lying underneath you with the shaft up. Since the square blade is flat and just slightly angular it fits underneath you without you barely feeling it. Now you can surf like a surfer in a prone position to get where you want to go in the water." She paddled to a spot in the water not far from the shore, I followed.

"Now it's time to find the 'sweet spot' on the board, and we do that by getting on to our knees. If you're too far back the nose of the paddle board will tilt to far upwards and the tail will sink. The sweet spot is in the middle of the board, you should feel balanced. Make a mental note of that spot so you will know where to put your feet."

I watched her do that and I copied her. I put my knees on the board and moved around on the board until I felt secure and steady. So far, so good. I looked at Mallory for the next step.

"Now that you have found the sweet spot on your knees I'm going to teach you how to use the paddle. You hold it like a canoe paddle, with your right hand on top, left hand on bottom. Paddle on one side, then switch hands and paddle on the other side. See? It's easy! One of the common mistakes people make when paddle boarding is using the paddle the wrong way. It may look easier to paddle with the blade scooping the water, but it's the opposite. The angle needs to point forward. Let's practice paddling on our knees a bit so you can get the hang of it before you stand."

We paddled around in circles paddling on both sides until I started to feel comfortable. This part was easy, but also a definite work out. Mallory asked if I was ready to stand up, I nodded yes.

"O.K. Your doing great Rayne. To stand up you put your paddle across the front of the board then place your feet on the sweet spot keeping your hips low. Grab the paddle in your hands and rise slowly. The key is to stay low and keep your knees slightly bent. If you stand straight up you'll fall off. Speaking of which, if you find yourself falling, don't fall on the board, fall away from it. Swim to your board first, then get your paddle. Also, keep your feet in the same position, don't put one in front of the other because it will put you off balance."

Mallory gracefully stood up and found her balance. "Your turn." She said.

I slowly (and shakily!) did as she did, keeping my body low and knees bent, feet in the same position. To my utter surprise I was able to eventually stand up without falling!

"That's it, Rayne, good job!" Mallory encouraged me. "Notice how I keep my arms straight away from my body, with one hand at the top of the paddle and the other farther down. Use your core, not your arms to paddle, and paddle in a downward and back motion. To turn, paddle on one side only. Once you get comfortable I'll teach you how to paddle from the back."

I did as she did and started to move around the water. I began to glide through the water, slow and steady. I could do this! I felt the warmth of the mid-day Florida sun on my body while simultaneously enjoying the sweet relief of cool spring water wind all around me. It felt glorious.

"I can't believe I'm doing this, Mallory! It's not so hard!" I yelled.

Not surprisingly I spoke to soon. Two seconds later I crashed and burned, falling in the water backside first. When I surfaced I saw Jenzy nearby in her kayak, and Mallory was sitting on her board giggling.

"How's the water feel, Rayne?" Jenzy asked me.

"Why don't you join me and find out for yourself?" I laughed too, after I spit out the water in my mouth I just about choked on when I fell. I swam back to my board.

"Sounds like a great idea!" Jenzy jumped in the water. "It feels great Mallory, jump in!"

Mallory joined us in the water. We floated around enjoying the refreshing spring water for a few minutes before getting back on our paddle boards and kayak. We spent the rest of the afternoon hanging out paddling around the blue waters. After many falls in the water, I'm proud to say that I, Rayne Lanecastor, could now paddle board with the best of them. My mom would love that.

22: Romeo & Juliet

I woke up Monday morning with slightly sore arm muscles and a big time interest/love for paddle boarding and kayaking. I decided to do both as much as possible whenever I could find the time. Right now I was anxious to get back to work at the Wildlife Academy. It was still dark when we got started. I joined everybody in the Wildlife Building to see where I would be scheduled to work, wondering who my partner would be. As I scanned the schedule I heard a familiar voice behind me.

"Looks like it's my lucky day. We're partners at the Aviary."

I felt a surge of happiness bubble up as I realized it was Maverick's pleasantly deep voice. It has been so long since I felt genuinely happy, I decided to let myself take it in and just feel it. It was a refreshing change of pace to be honest.

"Hi Maverick, good morning." I surprised myself by sounding cool, calm, and collected. Meanwhile, I was slightly freaking out, but in a good way.

"Are you ready to get started?" He asked.

"More than ready, Mav. It's going to be a great day."

We went to the wildlife kitchen to pick up the morning diets for the Aviary animals then we placed them in a large work cart along with two rakes, trash bags, and some scrub brushes. The work cart had two large wheels and could be easily pulled to wherever you were working. Maverick did the heavy lifting to push it to the Aviary for us. Clearly chivalry was alive and kicking in Mavericks world. When we reached the Wildlife Walk I was awestruck once again by its natural beauty. Seeing it by the dawn of the day made me stop in my tracks, it was that stunning.

"It's breathtakingly beautiful." I quietly murmured.

"Almost as beautiful as you, Rayne." Maverick's eyes stared directly in mine. I stared back, basking in the compliment he just gave me. He thinks I'm beautiful??? Hearing Maverick say that filled me with happiness *again* but this time it wasn't a surge it was a *tsunami* of happy feelings reaching from my head to my toes. I was frantically searching for the right words to say back to him when he dropped his gaze. He picked up the cart handle again and started moving which saved me from having to say anything. We spent the morning laying out the diets and cleaning the habitats. Maverick was a wealth of knowledge about the animals, he knew so much about them. I soaked up his knowledge thirstily, I wanted to know everything. He pointed out the different species of birds in the Aviary, the many different kinds of Herons, Egrets, Ibis, and Wood Storks (a large white bird with a dark bald face and neck and curved bill that is endangered.) I especially liked the birds called the Roseate Spoonbills, lightly pink feathered birds with bills that were shaped like a long handled spoon! Florida sure has the most delightful array of gracefully feathered birds. Then there were the Flamingos. I had heard about Flamingos my whole life, but seeing them in person was quite a different story. They were dark pink, elongated and gangly. They meandered around in the streams of the Aviary squawking in communication with each other. Some stood there, with one leg tucked up under its body, soaking up the warm sun. Others ate out of the pans of flamingo diet (yes, it's a thing) that Maverick and I had placed in bins around their habitat. They were fun to watch.

I worked for an hour hosing off the Aviary boardwalk (birds are lovely but their poop is not!) I spent that time contemplating my new life circumstances. I never would have imagined myself living in Florida, working with wildlife, making new friendships, and developing what could only be described as a major crush on a very handsome and interesting guy. I mentally thanked my mom for sending me here. Despite my burgeoning happiness I could not quite get past the still deep heaviness I felt missing her. Sadness that felt like a knife to my stomach, causing real physical pain. Before I succumbed to that hurt I reminded myself of my promise to her to choose happiness over sadness, and I remembered her telling me she would not be happy in heaven if she knew I was miserable. With that memory came a small smile, and I blinked my rapidly forming tears away. My mother wanted me to embrace life, so I will. I finished my job cleaning the boardwalk. I stood back, admiring my clean handiwork.

"Looks good, Rayne." I heard Maverick say. I looked to see where he was. He was sitting on a bench nearby drinking water, I was so immersed in my thoughts while cleaning I hadn't seen him take a seat there.

"Thanks, Mav, and thanks for all the knowledge you shared with me about the wildlife here. I learned so much." I gave him a genuinely happy smile.

"Oh there it is, a smile! While you were working you seemed so sad and serious. I was wondering why...do you want to sit for a minute? Let's take a break. I want to tell you a wildlife story."

He handed me my S'well water bottle that I had placed in the work cart earlier. I sat next to him taking a long drink of thirst quenching cold water. I noticed we were sitting right in front of the Whooping Crane exhibit.

"Have you heard the story about Romeo & Juliet?" He asked me.

"I don't know very much, only a little that my uncle told me when he was giving me a tour. You're talking about Levi and Peepers, right? He told me they have a special love story."

"That's right, they do. Very special. Their story proves that nothing can stop two star crossed lovers from being together, no matter what obstacles come their way. Levi-AKA-Romeo, would never give up trying to be with his true love. Would you like to hear it?"

"Yes, please!" I replied, then Maverick proceeded to tell me the most wonderful love story ever.

"It all began when Levi flew over Peeper's exhibit at the park while he was part of Operation Migration, a long migration from Wisconsin to Florida that a group of cranes make flying behind an Ultra light airplane each year. They fly to a Refuge area near the park where they spend the summer months. Levi got his name because his leg band identification number is 501-like the jeans. Peepers got her name because of the vocalization noises she makes. She came to the park as part of program to educate the public about the Whooping Cranes and their near extinction status. It was very difficult for your uncle to get the permits and convince the Whooping Crane Foundation to allow her to reside at this park, but he did it. He had to design and build this exhibit for her. Since the Whooping Crane foundation already flew the cranes here every year it was a perfect fit. I tell you, it was a real big deal your uncle got her here, because you can only see them in just a few zoological institutions around the United States, they are so rare. I helped build this habitat."

"Wow. Impressive, Maverick, you should be so proud!"

"Thanks, I am. Here's where the story gets interesting. Do you believe in love at first sight, Rayne?"

I nodded yes. Boy, do I ever! I thought, gazing at him.

"So do I, and apparently so does Levi. He flew over Peepers exhibit, heard her sweet vocalizations and that was all it took. He left his migrating companions, promptly flying down directly into her exhibit."

"How romantic." I sighed.

"That's why he got the nickname Romeo. Unfortunately for the two love birds, Levi couldn't stay. The Migration Foundation experts came and got him, taking him back to the flock which was now at the refuge. What they didn't expect was that Levi was not having it. He had found his mate, and he was going to be with her. Over the course of a year Levi continued to fly back to Peepers. Each time he did, the foundation team would come back, dress up like a crane, capture him, and take him back to the refuge. You have to understand their position, a male breeding crane is worth his weight in gold. The Foundation is dedicated to bringing his specie back from the brink of extinction. Did you know that Whooping Cranes mate for life?"

"No, I had no idea. So what happened? He obviously got to stay, because I'm looking at his spectacular self right now. They are such handsome birds, they look perfect for each other!" I was eager to hear the ending to this love story.

"After about 10 visits to Peepers the Operation Migration team finally caved. An agreement was made with your uncle to let Levi stay. They all knew that Romeo had found his lifelong mate, his Juliet, Peepers. Do you want to hear the best part Rayne?"

"Yes!" I replied eagerly, loving this story.

"Peepers has made a nest, and has laid her first egg. Do you see her nest over there? We candled the egg, unfortunately it's not fertile but it's a start. They could eventually be one of the first pair of Whooping Cranes to successfully breed in a zoological setting."

"What does candled the egg mean?" I was curious.

"It's when you put a special light up to the egg to see if there is an embryo developing inside." He explained.

"And they lived happily ever after! What a great story, Maverick!"

"The moral of the story is this, I think." He gave me a soulful stare and it was like a jolt to every one of the nerves I had in my body. How could

I feel that feeling just by a look? It wasn't just that Maverick was so beyond cute, it was his passion that was so attractive. "Sometimes animals -just like people- are destined to be together and are true soulmates. I admire Levi and his devotion. What about you?"

"It's the most romantic story I have ever heard, Maverick. Levi and Peepers really are Romeo and Juliet!" I glanced at the 'destined to be together' crane couple, deciding that life can be pretty amazing, just like the person sitting next to me. I turned to face Maverick. I knew in that moment that he was going to kiss me. I leaned in and just when his lips almost touched mine we heard a voice calling out to us from behind, a syrupy voice I recognized immediately as Serafina's.

"There you are Maverick I've been looking everywhere for you!" She said in her best pouty voice. "It's lunch time and you promised to eat with me today!"

I backed up immediately and quickly. Maverick cursed silently under his breath.

"What I remember Serafina is that you said we were all ordering pizza and eating together."

I stood up to leave, facing her.

"Hi Serafina. Nice to see you. Thank you Maverick, for everything. Especially the story."

I left before anyone could say anything more. Once again Serafina got what she wanted, and it wasn't eating lunch with me. I went home for lunch, I didn't see Maverick again for the rest of the day. Later that night before I went to bed I researched Whooping Cranes. I used my iPad to write a page about them to add to my new wildlife information notebook.

Whooping Cranes

Scientific Classification

Kingdom: Animalia

Phylum: Chordata

Class: Aves

Order: Gruiformes

Family: Gruidae

Genus: Grus

The Whooping Crane (Grus americana), the tallest North American bird, is an endangered crane species named for it's whooping sound. In 2003, there were about 153 pairs of whooping cranes. Along with the Sandhill Crane, it is one of only two crane species found in North America. The Whooping Crane's lifespan is estimated to be 22 to 24 years in the wild. After being pushed to the brink of extinction by unregulated hunting and loss of habitat to just 21 wild and two captive Whooping Cranes by 1941, conservation effects have led to a limited recovery.

Description

An adult Whooping Crane is white with a red crown and a long, dark, pointed bill. Immature Whooping Cranes are cinnamon brown. While in flight, their long necks are kept straight and their long dark legs trail behind. Adult Whooping Cranes black wing tips are visible during flight.

The Species can stand up to 5 feet and have a wing span of 7.5 feet. Males weigh on average about 15 pounds while females average 14. The Whooping Crane is endangered mainly as a result of habitat loss, although Whoopers are also still illegally shot despite this being subject to substantial financial penalties and possible prison time.

Vocalizations

Their calls are loud and can carry several kilometers. They express "guard calls" for warning their partner about any potential danger. The crane pair will jointly call a "unison call" in a very rhythmic and impressive way after waking in the early morning, after courtship, and when defending their territory.

Habitat

Wood Buffalo National Park in Alberta, Canada, and the surrounding area was the last remnant of the former nesting habitat of the Whooping Crane Summer Range. However, with the recent Whooping Crane Eastern Partnership Reintroduction Project, Whooping Cranes nested naturally for the first time in 100 years in the Necedah National Wildlife Refuge in central Wisconsin, USA. Breeding populations winter along the Gulf coast of Texas, USA, near Rockport on the Aransas National Wildlife Refuge and along Sunset Lake in Portland, Matagorda Island, Isla San Jose, and portions of the Lamar Peninsula and Welder Point, which is on the east side of San Antonia Bay. They nest on the ground, usually on a raised area in a marsh. The female lays 1 or 2 eggs, usually in late-April to mid-May. The incubation period is 29-31 days. Both parents brood the young, although the female is more likely to directly tend to the young. Usually no more than one young bird survives in a season. The parents often feed the young for 6-8 months after birth and the terminus of the offspring-parent relationship occurs after about 1 year.

Diet

These birds forage while walking in shallow water or in fields, sometimes probing with their bills. They are omnivorous and more inclined to animal material than most other cranes. In their Texas wintering grounds, they feed on various crustaceans, mollusks, fish (such as eel), berries, small reptiles and aquatic plants. Potential foods of breeding birds in summer include frogs, small rodents, smaller birds, fish, aquatic insects, crayfish, clams, snails, aquatic tubers, and berries. Waste grain, including wheat, barley, and corn, is an important food for migrating cranes, but Whooping Cranes don't swallow gizzard stones and digest grains less efficiently than Sandhill Cranes.

23: Two kittens of a very different kind

The saying "Time flies when your having fun" couldn't be more true. Another week flew by as I worked with wildlife at the park during the day, mainly in the Aviary cleaning lots of gross bird poop and feeding hundreds of birds. I was fast becoming a duck expert, there are 15 different duck species paddling along in the huge Aviary man-made pond. I also was beginning to be able to identify many different kinds of wading birds; the dancing White Egrets (large & small), Cormorants, the endangered Wood Storks, as well as the many different colored and exquisitely fancy feathered kinds of herons.

In the late afternoons after work I would paddle board or kayak on the Homosassa River near my new home because I had fallen in love with doing both. I was also beginning to recognize and get to know the different manatees that lived in the Blue Springs area near the park. It's unfortunately true that you can identify most manatees by their scars on their body. There are also a few with trackers attached around the base of their large, paddle shaped tails. If a manatee had a tracker then it was most likely rescued and released after it was rehabilitated or treated for injuries. You could actually track their migrations around Florida waters on a computer. That was pretty neat, I thought. There is one manatee named Charlie who zips around all over Florida waters both fresh and salt. He was originally brought to the wildlife park years ago because he almost died during an unusual cold spell for Florida. He recovered in the year round spring temperatures of 72 degree Homosassa Springs water, and was subsequently tagged then released. Charlie liked to travel, but according to my uncle he always comes back and stays for awhile. I'd also become very fond of Rose and her adorable calf, which I privately named Rosetta. Rose is friendly and curious by nature, she loves to hang around my dock and suck on the ropes attached to the pontoon boat and kayaks docked there. So weird. Quite often she'd come up to my kayak (she liked it better than a paddle board- not sure why!) to let me scratch her back and rub her belly as she'd turn upside down. Rosetta liked to grab my hands with her front flippers so I could rub her cute little whiskers around her mouth. Once again I could not believe this was my new life. As great as the week was it got better Saturday morning, because that morning I became acquainted with two of the most adorable yet drastically different kittens, one who was once wild, the other---not so much.

"Wake up Rayne!!! Mallory is here and she has something awesome to show us! She is on the porch with mom and dad." Aiden came flying in to my room after knocking.

"O.K. I'll be right down, Aiden." I hurriedly got dressed then raced downstairs. I walked out to the porch and I saw everyone sitting around a basket full of some seriously cute kittens. There were five of them, they all had silver/white fluffy fur with little spots of black fur patches around the tips of their ears and around their feet as well.

"Kittens!" I squealed as I quickly sat down with everyone else and starting playing with them. They were so soft and silky, and the smallest one of all would not leave my side, wanting to sit on my lap while purring contentedly as I pet her. Mallory told me the one I was holding was a girl and the runt of the litter. The rest were all males.

"I have posted a note in the volunteer building offering them up for adoption, I've already received many offers. Naturally I'll make sure they go to really good homes." She said.

My Aunt Beth looked at me like she was about to burst with excitement.

"Looks like you've made a new friend, Rayne. Do you like her?"

"Oh I adore her Aunt Beth, she's just perfection!" I said as the little kitten purred away.

"Well we are so glad to hear you like her, Rayne, because she's all yours. Bart and I discussed it, and if you want, we want you to have her."

I looked at everyone around me and they were all smiling at me. Tears of happiness flooded my eyes. **#happytearsaresomuchbetterthansadtears!**

"Yes I want her, very much! Thank you, Thank you, Thank you! I have never owned a cat before, I promise I will take the very best care of her." I hugged my new kitten gazing into her large blue eyes. "I will call her Luna, because she reminds me of a silvery midnight moon."

"That's perfect, Rayne, I'm so glad you want her. She is my favorite and now I can come visit her all the time." Mallory said.

"Will you help me play with her Aiden?" I asked him.

"I sure will, Rayne. It will be good practice for me, Mom and dad have promised to get us our very own dog soon. When we do we are going to adopt one from the local Animal Shelter."

Mallory said she had to go show off the kittens to the volunteers so she left. My aunt said that we had to go to the pet store to get all the supplies a kitten would need, such as a food and water bowl set, food, kitty litter box, and a cat collar with an I.D. Tag. Mallory and Maverick's mom already started the necessary vaccinations for the kittens and would continue to give them any veterinarian care they might need. I asked Aiden to watch Luna while we went to the pet store, he happily obliged. Little did we know that later on that afternoon another kitten would come our way, only this time the "Kitten" would be a highly endangered, unfortunately orphaned, Florida Panther cub.

Uncle Bart received an urgent phone call from the Wildlife Staff telling him he needed to come to the Wildlife Building as soon as he possibly could. Two Florida Fish and Wildlife Biologists were there seeking help for a young Florida Panther kitten that had just been found in the Florida Panther National Wildlife Refuge in Collier County. They told my Uncle Bart the kitten was found in a matted down area of sawgrass and was unresponsive. It's body temperature was dangerously low and there was no mother around to be found. Uncle Bart told them he was on his way.

"Would you like to tag along, Rayne?" He asked. Naturally, I said yes.

There was a group of people clustered around the examining table when we got to the Wildlife Building hospital, but my eyes only saw one person, and his name was Maverick Greene. He was standing next to his mom trying to comfort the softly mewing little panther as she examined it. His eyes were intently focused on the kitten with pure love and admiration. I realized my eyes were probably doing the same looking at Maverick. He was compassionate, good to know. The panther kitten was adorable, his fur looked like soft beige cashmere dotted with dark brown spots all over its body. It's eyes were the color of light blue spring water. Ms. Greene said it was a male, that it was approximately 7 days old, in need of hydration immediately, and treated for malnourishment. My uncle said to do whatever was necessary to save its life, then he left with the Biologists to talk about the future of the panther kitten. That's when Maverick noticed me, bestowing on me the same look of admiration that he had given the panther cub.

"Hey Rayne, isn't he great? Come closer, it's not everyday you get to gaze at such a spectacular endangered specie. I took a few steps closer to observe the tiny ball of fur, who at the moment was being hooked up to an I.V. Bag full of fluids administered by Mavericks mom.

"Will he make it, Ms. Greene?" I quietly asked her.

"I'm going to do everything I can, Rayne, to make him better. The next few days will be critical. It's going to take round the clock care. We are going to have some sleepless nights, Maverick." She said to her son.

"I'm down for that mom, I'm all in. I'm honored to get this opportunity."

A thought occurred to me just then. I asked them both a question.

"Would you mind if I journaled the rehabilitation process? I'm very organized and promise to record everything accurately."

Ms. Greene gave me a look of respect. "I think that is a fine idea, Rayne, and Maverick and I can give you the details of his recovery and eating process. You can be a liaison to the volunteers and public with the information. I think it will be a great learning experience for you. It's fine with me."

"I'm down for that, too." Maverick agreed. "It's a great idea."

And just like that I became responsible for two very drastically different yet equally wonderful felines.

Florida Panther
Scientific Classification

Kingdom: Animalia

Phylum: Chordata

Class: Mammalia

Order: Carnivore

Family: Felidae

Genus: Puma

Species: P. con color

The Florida Panther is an endangered subspecies of cougar (Puma concolor) that lives in forests and swamps of southern Florida in the United States. This species is also known as the cougar, mountain lion, and puma. In Florida it is known exclusively known as the panther. Florida Panthers are usually found in pinelands, hardwood hammocks, and mix swamp forests. Males can weigh up to 160 pounds and live within a range that includes the Big Cypress National Preserve, Everglades National Park, and the Florida Panther National Wildlife Refuge. This population, the only unequivocal cougar representative in the eastern United States, currently occupies 5% of its historic range. In the 1970's, there were an estimated 20 Florida Panthers in the wild. Once nearly extinct, the Florida Panthers are making a slow comeback, today there is approximately 150 to 200 Florida Panthers left in the wild. They are one of the rarest and most endangered mammals in the world. Even though they are making a comeback that number of panthers is not a sustainable population size. The Florida Panther is currently listed as endangered and is protected under the endangered species act. In 1982, the Florida Panther was chosen as the Florida state animal.

Description

Florida Panthers are spotted at birth and typically have blue eyes. As the panther grows the spots fade and the coat becomes completely tan while the eyes typically take on a yellow hue. The panther's underbelly is a creamy white, with black tips on the tail and ears. Florida Panthers lack the ability to roar, and instead make distinct sounds that include whistles, chirps, growls, hisses, and purrs. Florida Panthers are mid-sized for the species, being smaller than cougars from Northern and Southern climes but larger than the cougars from the neotropics. Adult female Florida Panthers weigh from 64-100 pounds.

Diet

The Florida Panther is a large carnivore whose diet consists of small animals like hares, mice, and waterfowl but also larger animals like deer, wild boar, and even the American Alligator.

Early Life

Panther kittens are born in dens created by their mothers, often in dense scrub. The dens are chosen based on a variety of factors, including prey availability, and have been observed in an array of habitats. Kittens will spend the first 6-8 weeks of life in those dens, dependent on their mother. In the first 2-3 weeks, the mother will spend most of her time nursing the kittens; after this period, she will spend more time away from the den, to wean the cubs and to hunt prey to bring to the den. Once they are old enough to leave the den, they will hunt in the company of their mother. Male panthers will not be encountered frequently during this time, as female and male panthers generally avoid each other outside of breeding. Kittens are usually 2 months old when they begin hunting with their mothers, and 2 years old when they begin to hunt and live on their own.

Threats

The Florida Panther has a natural predator, the alligator. Humans also threaten it through poaching and wildlife control measures. Besides predation, the biggest threat to their survival is human encroachment. The two highest causes of mortality for individual Florida Panthers are automobile collisions and territorial aggression between panthers. When these incidents injure the panthers, federal and Florida wildlife officials take them to conservation and rehabilitation facilities for recovery and rehabilitation until they are well enough to be released and reintroduced.

Primary threats to the population as a whole include habitat loss, habitat degradation, and habitat fragmentation. Southern Florida is a fast-developing area and certain developments threaten prime panther habitats.

24: Yuma and Luna

For the next two weeks I filled my days and nights with kitten care and kayaking. When I wasn't learning Animal Care at the Wildlife Academy I devoted the rest of my time to the care of my new kitten, Luna, and to keeping records of the Florida Panther cub, named Yuma by Maverick and the rest of the Animal Care staff. "Yuma" means 'Son of the Chief' and is an American Indian word. In my spare time I discovered I loved kayaking around the Blue Springs and Homosassa River because it brought me peace and serenity as well as adventure. My uncle and aunt were now comfortable with me doing this alone as long as I stayed close to home and kept my phone, whistle, and life jacket on me at all times. I was also able to take pictures if I kayaked. I splurged on a waterproof otter box for my phone so I could do so and not worry about ruining my phone with water in case I accidentally fell in. Every time I was on the water I'd see or experience something wonderful~ like my continued contact with Rose & Rosetta, or being able to witness the most visually stunning sunset I'd ever laid my eyes upon. In fact, when the sun would start to set, I knew it was time to go home. I felt like I could do all my deep thinking and do it clearly when I was paddling through the soothing waters. Occasionally Mallory would join me but for the most part I enjoyed going alone. Maverick told me he wanted to join me one day soon but he was so busy raising Yuma and waking up in the late hours to feed him that it left him too exhausted to do anything else but eat and take short naps. I was loving every minute taking notes and keeping a journal about Yuma's recovery and growth. I really admired watching Maverick's dedication. Under Mavericks care, Yuma was starting to thrive. Maverick was bottle feeding Yuma KMR (kitten milk replacement) every 2-3 hours and he would text me after every feeding how many ounces he'd consume. Yuma had finally turned from a weak and emaciated Panther cub into a fat and healthy one. Soon Yuma would start eating a more carnivorous meal, and on his own. For now though, he had to be fed and nursed much like he would by his mother. In addition to record keeping information about Yuma I also had to video record his progress~a job I was honored to do and took very seriously. I did this usually in the early morning before everyone else showed up for the Academy, it was nice to have quiet time with Maverick and his mother and of course the magnificently adorable Yuma. Getting up early while it was still dark didn't bother me at all, in fact, I enjoyed it. I loved the cool Florida early mornings much better than the hot and humid afternoons. Today Yuma was playing with stuffed animals much like he would with cub mates. I could not help but giggle and laugh out loud at the cub's silly antics. I was alone for the time being because Maverick and his mother left to go get us breakfast. In fact I was so absorbed in the moment that when I heard a voice behind me say "Well isn't this a sight to behold!" I literally jumped right out of my skin I was so startled! I placed my hand over my heart turning slowly around. What I saw was the sleepy looking Drew MacArthur, and he was smiling at me brighter than the sun about to rise.

25: Drew MacArthur

"**D**rew!" I kind of yelped with a slightly shaky voice. "I didn't hear you come in the hospital. Wow, You startled me."

"Sorry love, I didn't mean to scare you. I just woke up and came to the kitchen to grab some coffee when I saw the lights on in the hospital and heard some captivating laughter. I was intrigued so here I am. I see it's Yuma that has provoked your delight. Lucky panther."

"It's alright Drew, my heart is recovering right now as we speak. I forgot you and Serafina live here in the building. Yuma's glorious, isn't he?" I asked while putting Yuma back into his cozy pen.

"He sure is Rayne, he's a handsome little devil. In Africa we have Leopards. Yuma reminds me of them."

"Do you miss being home?"

"Yes and no. South Africa is spectacular, refined yet wild, exotic yet cultured. Desmond Tutu and Nelson Mandela referred to it as a Rainbow Nation because of its multicultural diversity. I miss my family but the chance to stay in America and further my education is too important to pass up. I can see myself living here for a long time. I want the best education I can get so I can combine my two passions, working with wildlife and traveling the world."

"That's awesome, Drew. I admire your passion."

"What about you Rayne? What's your story?"

"My story is being written right now, Drew. It's a work in progress. Nothing you'd find exciting I'm afraid."

"You couldn't be more wrong, Rayne. You're a contradiction I'd like to figure out. Sometimes you look so sad and serious. Makes me want to make you smile. And just now your pure delight and genuine laughter pulled me closer to you like a moth to a flame. You intrigue me, I can see what he finds so fascinating about you."

The last part he said so quietly I barely heard him. Drew looked at me with pure appreciation. I'm not gonna lie, I liked it. It didn't suck. Good thing Mallory saved the day by walking in the room looking for me, easing my social awkwardness by giving me something else to focus on.

"Well there you are Rayne! I've been looking all over this building for you! Hi Drew! Good morning! My mom just brought everyone breakfast-bagels, donuts, and coffee! Are you two hungry?"

"As a matter of fact I'm starved Mallory, and Drew was just saying he wanted coffee. Perfect timing."

In more ways than one, I thought to myself.

"Well then, allow me to escort you to the breakfast hall, ladies." Drew proclaimed, linking his arms through ours. "A morning feast awaits!"

26: Manatee Water Rescue 911

Breakfast with the wildlife crew was fun and full of laughter. We talked about the day's work ahead that needed done, sharing any information about animals in our care. I loved the feeling of being and belonging to a team with the same goals and interests. As we enjoyed our breakfast, the Wildlife Staff received a phone call about an injured manatee in the river close to the park.

"A woman has called from her house on the river saying a manatee seems to be in distress." Ms. Greene relayed to us. "I have called Bart and we have formed a rescue team consisting of Maverick, Drew, and Sheri. Bart is getting the boat ready now." She noticed my video camera. "Rayne will you come and document the rescue?"

"Yes of course!" I followed everyone to the MOO building to get our wetsuits.

When we all had our suits on we raced to the pontoon rescue boat that is specifically outfitted for rescues. It was big enough to accommodate a stretcher for the manatee if it was injured. Maverick showed me the specially designed lift for raising one out of the water if necessary. My uncle drove the boat while the boys kept a look out.

"Sheri, why would there be a net in the river and what kind of net would it be?" I was curious to know.

"It's illegal in Florida to use any nets besides a casting net to fish, has been for a very long time." She answered. "It's probably going to be a gill net, a net which is named for trapping a fish in the net by its gills. The gill net was popular with the local fishermen here to mainly catch mullet. But the nets are very destructive and Floridians voted on an amendment to ban them outright. They are especially prohibited near residential areas, which is where we are heading. I hope the manatee has enough strength to hold on!" She looked worried.

"Me too, Sheri!" I closed my eyes and prayed. Lord please hear my prayer, please help us to save the poor manatee! I hoped he heard my prayer because minutes later I heard Drew shout "I see it! Stop the boat!" My uncle stopped the boat immediately. I saw the manatee and I could see it was completely entangled! I grabbed my camera to start filming. The manatee was struggling-it kept sinking down under the water. It was desperately trying to come to the top to catch a breath.

"It appears to be in distress guys, time is of the essence." Sheri said.

"The net is huge, we will have to physically remove it." Uncle Bart added.

Everyone but Sheri and I dove into the water. When they reached the manatee the rescue began in ernest. Ms. Greene went to soothe the manatee while my uncle, Maverick, and Drew started the difficult job of cutting the large heavy net with knives to release it. The goal was to free her first, then take the net out of the water. I could not believe how badly the manatee was wrapped up in it, the poor thing must have frantically tried to free itself to no avail! I heard Ms. Greene say it must be completely exhausted because it was so still, that she was basically holding its head above water. Ten very long minutes later I heard a jubilant cry from Maverick. "That's it! It's free!"

I was looking at them through the lens of the camera when something about the manatee caught my eye. Before I could react to what I saw I had to help Maverick, Drew, and Sheri place the offending net on to the boat. When we finished we looked toward the manatee, my uncle was still holding her while Ms.Greene examined her body for any injuries. It wasn't moving. My uncle kept talking to the manatee as if to encourage her to fight for her life. It was heartbreaking! I couldn't stop myself, I jumped into the water to join them. Their expressions were very grim.

"I don't think it's going to make it, Rayne." He said.

"No! I don't accept that! Look it's Rose, Maverick! Do you see her scar? I noticed on the camera but I wasn't sure...now I am! Where is her calf? Where is Rosetta?" We all looked around.

"Look she's here! Over there!" Drew pointed to a spot nearby.

A sigh of relief escaped me when I spotted her too. I refocused my attention to Rose. I stroked her long back, talking to her. "Snap to it Rose! You can do it! Stay here for your calf, she needs you! Please don't leave us, please don't go!" I continued to stroke her while my uncle held her face up. I was crying, I didn't care who saw. I wrapped my arms around her as best I could, willing her to live. We stayed like that for what seemed like an eternity, but was actually not long at all. It was then that I felt something nudge me in the water. It was Rosetta. "Look mama! Your baby!" I moved so that Rose could see/feel her near. I guided the baby calf to her mother until their noses touched, whiskers to whiskers. "Rose, it's your baby!" Just then I felt a sudden movement in the water. It was Rose's tail. she had moved it!

"Look Uncle Bart, she moved!" I jubilantly proclaimed.

"She is, she's moving now." He said with a huge smile on his face as he let her go. Rose took a deep breath of air then slowly started to swim a short distance away with her baby. The most wonderful feeling of relief mixed with euphoria surged through every part of my body.

"You have a way with animals Rayne." Ms. Greene said to me. "It seemed like you were actually communicating with Rose, and that Rose was listening. It was very special."

"I agree with Joni." Uncle Bart said. "Well done, Rayne. You are officially a Wildlife Warrior! Now let's get in the boat and watch her until some volunteers can come here and relieve us. They will take turns observing her behavior. I don't think it's necessary at this point to take her out of her habitat to the Manatee Hospital, especially since she has her calf." They swam to the boat, I reluctantly followed. I looked back once more on the now moving together manatees. I said another prayer to God, this time a prayer of thanks. We boarded the boat and we all high fived each other and hugged. It was a successful rescue!

The rescue of Rose the manatee brought me profound clarity about my future. I now knew without a shadow of a doubt that I was going to devote my entire life to being a Wildlife Rescuer, Rehabilitator, and Educator. My uncle called me a Wildlife Warrior and I liked the sound of that. It was like *another* bolt of lightning had struck me but this time it struck my soul, igniting a fire deep inside of me never to be extinguished.

27: Beach Bound Birthdays

I t was an emotionally charged week for me but I wouldn't have changed one thing. I was super stoked that Rose was alive to raise her calf and that was all that really mattered. I was ready for a fun filled weekend and I had something very exciting to look forward to-a party at the beach on Sunday celebrating Maverick & Mallory's 16th birthdays. Their mom rented a party bus to take us to a beach on the gulf called Pine Island. It's been a long time since I was at a beach, I couldn't wait to lie in the warm sun on the warm sand. The whole Wildlife Jr. Ranger crew was coming so it was sure to be a good time. I was currently shopping with Jenzy because I needed a new bathing suit and we wanted to buy birthday gifts for Maverick and Mallory. My Aunt Beth drove us to the mall then left for a couple of hours to do some errands.

"Where do you want to start?" Jenzy asked.

"I'd like to go to the store 'Things Remembered' to look at gifts for the twins. I want to get something special for the both of them that can be engraved."

I loved everything in the store. I zeroed in on the bracelets for Mallory, finding one that was just perfect for her. It was made of strips of dark red leather adorned with shimmering red glass beads that were intertwined, with a gold heart charm dangling from it. It was earthy and sparkling with bling at the same time, just like Mallory's personality. I decided to get the pendant engraved with a girly cursive "M" on it.

"It's gorgeous!" Jenzy's enthusiasm matched mine. "We will have to go to the vintage dress shop to get something to match with it. You know how much she loves Vintage!"

"That's a great idea, Jenzy. What about this for Maverick?" I showed Jenzy a shiny black military style dog tag necklace with a long black leather braided cord. "I can get it engraved with his name on one side and his birth date on the other."

"It's dope. He will dig it, Rayne."

"O.K. done." I purchased the gifts. The sales clerk said it would take an hour to engrave them, so we went to the vintage dress store that Jenzy wanted to shop at. The store was like stepping back in time, all of the clothes and accessories were from decades in the past, like the 50's, 60's, and 70's.

"*Eureka*!" Jenzy yelled. She showed me a very delicate Burgundy red short sleeve sweater made out of cashmere, the softest, most coziest fabric! What made it even more beautiful was the glass beaded, Jewel toned hummingbird perched upon its shoulder. It was exquisite, it would go perfectly with the bracelet I bought her.

"I love it. How much is it? It looks expensive." I asked.

"Luckily it's on sale, which means I can afford it. Sold!"

As she was paying for the sweater I continued to shop. There was something I had to check out. I was intrigued when I saw it sitting on a mannequin's head upon entering the store. It was a tan colored, straw fedora hat that I wanted to try on. It had a black fabric band around the base of it. I thought it would be perfect for sun protection while still being stylish. Best part was it was only $15. I adored it, had to have it. After another hour of shopping I found a black one piece bathing suit that was both comfortable and cute. Bonus, it matched my new hat. Jenzy took me to a make up store where she talked me into buying some waterproof mascara and berry tinted lip gloss. She bought eyeshadow from the brand Urban Decay for herself, colors that were edgy and sleek, like a shimmery silver and gun metal grey. The colors actually matched Mavericks new necklace, I observed. She said she wanted to perfect the "smokey eye" and even though I would probably never wear those colors, I couldn't wait to see what she did with them on herself. We picked up my newly engraved gifts for Maverick & Mallory then finished our shopping with a meal at the food court before heading home. The excitement and anticipation of what tomorrow would bring made me feel good to be alive, and I allowed the good feelings to enter my heart. It was a refreshing change of pace, happy feelings over sad, and I knew, without a shadow of a doubt, that my parents were damn proud of me.

28: Party Time

The next morning I looked out of my third story window to see a dazzlingly warm Florida sun beckoning to me, 'Rayne! Come enjoy my splendidly sparkling sunrays!' I bounded downstairs to eat a small breakfast with my new family that I was rapidly falling in love with, and to spend some quality time with my adorable cousin Aiden. He was drinking some orange juice, it looked so good I decided to join him. It tasted like liquid gold, it was delicious.

"Yummy!" I murmured.

"Mom just fresh squeezed it, it's good isn't it?" Aiden said.

Aunt Beth smiled. "Another reason to love Florida, right Rayne? Oranges are fresh and plentiful here. All year round. Are you hungry? I made French toast."

"Yes, but I'm so excited about going to the beach party I'm not sure how much I'll be able to eat!"

I tried the French Toast, then promptly devoured every single bit of it.

"You are going to have so much fun, Rayne! Joni has planned a wonderful party for the twins and since she's chaperoning it I feel comfortable knowing you'll be safe while having a good time. Wear sunscreen." Beth advised.

"I will and I'm wearing my new hat so that will help with shading me from the sun. I'll pack water in my bag too. Thanks for the caring advice. I appreciate it." I helped Aiden clean up our breakfast dishes then went back upstairs with a cup of coffee to wrap the gifts and get ready. The party bus would be picking us up at the Wildlife Building at noon, so I had some time to chill. I grabbed my iPad and sat on my bed. Luna curled up next to me purring contentedly while she napped. I opened up my notes application to read another letter from my mom. I just wanted to hear her voice, even if it was her written voice. I zeroed in on the perfect one to read before I left for the party.

"Here's a Hug"

Dearest wonderful daughter of mine, I may no longer be here physically but know that I am always in spirit! For those times when you miss me, need a hug from your mom, please just read this letter from me to you! The very best thing I did in my life was create you. You made my life complete, and made me feel like I accomplished something extraordinary. In my eyes, you are perfect. You are perfect, flaws and all. Don't ever forget that my love. So close your eyes, wrap your arms around yourself, and imagine me hugging you tight!!

The party bus pulled up to the Wildlife Building to pick us up and we all cheered. It was huge-all black, super sleek, and shiny. The interior of the bus was dark but there were bright blue LED lights strategically placed allowing just enough light to see everyone and everything, in a nightclub kind of way. Music was playing from hidden speakers, and a large flat screen T.V. was mounted from the ceiling at the very back of the bus. Best part was the air conditioning, because the whole interior felt deliciously cool. Josie said it was lit, I totally agreed, it *was* epic. Ms. Greene handed each of us a glass of sparkling cider to make a toast to the birthday boy and girl.

"We are all here today to celebrate the birthdays of my two wonderful kids, kids that I couldn't be more blessed to call my own. Maverick and Mallory, you deserve this day to be the best birthday you've ever had, because you are the best kids ever! I love you both with all my heart and soul! Thank you everyone else for coming, it makes this day even more special. Now let's get this party started!"

I looked around the party bus just enjoying the moment and taking in everyone sitting around me. There was the Birthday twins, Maverick and Mallory, Jenzy, Josie, Liam, Drew, and Serafina. My new friends. Except for Serafina, I couldn't count her as a friend. She seemed to dislike me and although that was baffling to me, it didn't bother me much either. I didn't know Liam very well, he is the quiet, intellectual type and mostly keeps to himself. Right now he was engrossed in a conversation with Jenzy and whatever she was saying to him must have been very interesting because she was moving her arms and hands up and down dramatically while laughing every so often. You couldn't watch her and not smile, her good vibes were contagious. Note to self, she likes him. I will have to see what's up with that. As I was mulling that over I felt more than saw someone staring at me intensely, as odd as that sounds. I glanced around the bus until my eyes locked on to Mavericks. There it was again! Female intuition. Crazy. He came over to me. I immediately forgot anyone else was on the bus.

"Why is it every time I look at you I feel I must know what it is you're thinking about that is making you display the most captivating smile?" Maverick asked me with his own captivating smile. **#ohmygoodness**

"I'm just enjoying the experience, trying to take it all in. I'm really grateful to be here, thanks for inviting me. Happy Birthday Maverick, I hope you get everything you want and have the best birthday ever!"

"It couldn't get any better than this right now, Rayne, except for one thing."

"What is that, Mav?" I was curious to know.

"A kiss, Rayne. In fact, I'm having a hard time not kissing you right here and now in front of everybody."

The way Maverick was staring at me made me wish we were alone and he could do just that. And once again, just like that, I was breathless. And speechless. And thankful that the party bus was as dark as a nightclub. I know I was three shades of red. Or maybe it was just getting a little warm in the bus? Amazingly enough, a minor miracle happened. I found the courage to say something bold.

"Next time we're alone, then." I challenged him. *OMG* was I *FLIRTING*???

His eyes widened and he smiled bigger than any smiley face emoji I had on my iPhone. He leaned in closer to me, immediately causing the now familiar goosebumps to form all over my body. It wasn't warm on the bus after all, because why else would I be close to shivering?

"Deal. Until then Rayne. Can't wait." With that promise made he got up and went to talk to Drew. For the second time within minutes I felt another person staring at me. This time it was coming from Serafina Serrano. Her arms were crossed and she looked furious. When she saw that I noticed her, she immediately glanced away and fake smiled at Josie, who was sitting next to her. Clearly she disliked me, but why? Was it jealousy? I wasn't sure, but I know I didn't like it one tiny little bit.

The rest of the day was filled with swimming, eating pizza and cake at the picnic tables, and dancing to music. The dancing was hysterical, with Maverick, Drew, and Liam breakdancing and the girls dancing the 80's dances. When Mallory did the 'Carlton' and 'Running Man' I laughed so hard it hurt. Naturally Serafina had to dance very seductively to one song, even I couldn't take my eyes off of her swinging hips. I was glad when that song was over! **#lol** The twins opened their gifts and loved them all. Mallory went crazy over her bracelet and sweater, Maverick immediately put on the necklace I gave him. It looked great on him, perfect. Just like the day. Currently Jenzy, Mallory and I were laying on our beach towels soaking in the sun talking girl talk while relaxing. I brought up Liam to Jenzy.

"You seemed to be really enjoying your conversation on the bus with Liam earlier, Jenzy. What's up with that?" I teased.

"I did. He's so interesting, Rayne. He's smart, sensitive, and sweet." She replied.

"I thought when I saw him smiling at you that he was very cute, too." I added.

"You really think so?" She asked.

"I think so too." Mallory joined in. He's *almost* as cute as Drew!" She giggled. "Drew is the cat's meow FOR SURE." Mallory looked over at Drew who at the moment was engaged in a conversation with Maverick and Serafina. Serafina was in her element, being the center of attention and loving it. She was wearing a red two piece bikini, she was a fire emoji personified. I realized that I was the jealous one at this moment.

"Check out miss need for attention." Mallory said, making me laugh.

"I was just thinking the same thing." I concurred. "The worst part is that she is so abnormally pretty."

"Pretty obnoxious." Jenzy said. We laughed together at that. That was some small consolation.

"Rayne did you know that when the Wildlife Ranger Academy ends there is a big party? It's called the Wildlife Ball. All of the park's employees and volunteers come to support and congratulate us." Mallory said.

"No. I had no idea."

Jenzy interrupted our conversation. "Look at Serafina, subtle she is not! Who is she flirting with, Maverick or Drew? I can't tell…"

What I saw made my heart sink a little. Both Maverick and Drew were completely captivated by whatever she was saying. I decided to go for a walk alone. I told the girls I was going to go for a walk to explore the beach. I wanted to walk fast away from that lovely vision. I felt better with each step I took from the jealousy I was experiencing. I didn't like that feeling one bit. It turned out to be a long walk. The beach was beautiful, I wanted to enjoy exploring it. I noticed so many different kinds of sea birds; Pelicans, Gulls, and Terns. I was almost all the way back to the party when I saw Maverick walking towards me.

"Welcome back, Miss Mysterious. I turn my back for one moment and you completely disappeared."

"I went for a walk, Mav, to do some exploring and thinking. It's special here."

"I agree." He replied. "I love your hat, it suits you and ....what's the word I'm thinking of....classy! You look classy."

I was so glad I purchased the hat. From now on it would be my lucky hat.

"Thank you Maverick, I just bought it. I'm glad you like it."

"I do, and I like you, too. Please don't disappear on me again. You don't want me to be unhappy on my Birthday do you?" He tried to look sad but only managed to make me giggle.

"Nope, we can't have that so I promise." I offered my hand for him to shake on it. He took it, holding it firmly. Then he did something that no other boy had ever done with me. He held my hand all the way back to the party. Despite that bit of unpleasantness earlier in the day watching Serafina flirt with Maverick, and despite Serafina's continual mean looks my way- the party at the beach turned out to be one of the best days. We went home tired, sunkissed, and ready for the challenging week ahead of us. I was more than ready for some hard work at the Academy, and deep down, but not too deep down, I allowed myself to hope for a moment alone with Maverick for a promised kiss. Best Birthday Beach Bash *ever!*

29: The Reptile House

I arrived at the Wildlife Building early Monday so I could catch up on some notes about Yuma. He was growing quickly, Maverick was weaning him off of KMR completely as he was starting to eat solid food. Soon enough the cub would be out of the nursery and living in a brand new habitat built exclusively for him. My uncle and the Wildlife Staff were working feverishly to complete it, it was coming along quite nicely. I finished catching up so I went to the Jr. Ranger bulletin board to see where I would be training for the next week. When I saw that I was going to train with Drew and Serafina in the Reptile House my heart sank.

1. I don't really like reptiles.
2. I don't really like Serafina.

Swell. Marvelous. This was going to be a very long week. I made myself a hot green tea with honey in the Wildlife Building kitchen while I waited for everybody to arrive. I couldn't wait to see the look on Serafina's face when she found out that she gets to spend some good quality reptile time with me. I'd be willing to bet she was going to be very displeased. In fact, I was beginning to think this assignment was going to be somewhat entertaining, and actually, appropriate. I thought Serafina was kind of reptilian in nature; cold blooded, sly, and vicious. I had a sneaking suspicion I might have to be more careful around her than the snakes. I decided I'd stick close to Drew, my momma didn't raise a fool. As it turned out, I was so right. Her face when discovering she was going to work with me was priceless. #Notahappycamper!

"Here at the Reptile House we have 20 different species of Florida snakes, 15 are not venomous, 5 are. You will not be working with the venomous snakes but you will be learning about them." Sheri the Wildlife Ranger explained to us. "We also have a variety of lizards and turtles, and there is also an exhibit of baby alligators that were born here at the park. When they get bigger they will go out to the gator exhibit. When you go home tonight I want you to study up on reptiles and Florida snakes. That will be your first assignment. After that, you will learn how to feed them, weigh them and clean their habitats. The venomous snake habitats are maintained by myself and the APM, Assistant Park Manager. Right now I will show you each habitat and talk to you about whatever reptile is in it. Take whatever notes you want, and don't hesitate to ask me any questions. Let's start with the gators."

With each passing habitat I was beginning to actually enjoy what I was learning. Reptiles are not so bad after all, they are definitely interesting. I was surprised when Sheri announced it was time to take a lunch break. Serafina took off like a rocket leaving me alone with Drew.

"Will you join me for lunch at the Wildlife Cafe?" Drew asked me.

"Sure. Maybe Mallory will be there. You like Mallory, don't you?" I asked him. He looked at me quizzically.

"Yes, she's a wonderful girl. But I wouldn't mind if it's just us, either."

That took me by surprise. What do I say to that?

"Oh, O.K." That's what I said to that.

We walked to the Wildlife Cafe and placed our orders, a chicken wrap with ranch dressing for me, a hotdog and fries for him. He insisted on paying, I only let him after he promised to let me pay next time. We took our food to an outside table shaded by a large umbrella. What followed was a pleasant, very enjoyable conversation dominated completely by Drew. He was extremely engaging, I found myself laughing easily at his stories about growing up in South Africa. I thought to myself that Mallory was so right about him, Drew really is the type of guy that walks in a room and instantly owns it. As a matter of fact, I was having such a good time I didn't notice we were about to be joined by Maverick, Mallory, and Serafina. Only one of them wore a smile on their face, and it wasn't the twins.

"Well *HELLO* you two, is this a date or can we join you?" Serafina gleefully inquired.

I almost choked on the Sprite I was drinking when she said that. I felt my face get warm with embarrassment. Not a good look I'd bet. Thankfully Drew answered that they definitely could join us. I spent the rest of our break wondering why I felt slightly guilty. It was just an innocent lunch for goodness sake. I didn't say much and that's mainly because Serafina kept gushing (ad nauseam, I might add) over Maverick. What started as a pleasant lunch quickly became the exact opposite. In my head I said 'thanks Serafina. You really suck' and that made me almost laugh out loud. It must have showed on my face because she stopped talking and called me out on it.

"Did I say something to amuse you, Rayne?"

"Everything you say I find amusing, Serafina, you're entertaining." Her eyes flashed with annoyance, and she frowned ever so slightly. I stood up. "It's been a great lunch but I have some serious studying to do. See you all later." With that declaration I walked as fast as I could away from the table. Score another victory for Serafina.

That night after dinner I made myself some hot chocolate then changed into my comfiest pajama's. I climbed into my equally comfortable bed to study. I searched the internet for some information about reptiles. Reptile knowledge here I come!

Reptiles

Reptiles, the class Reptilia, are an evolutionary grade of animals, comprising today's turtles, crocodilians, snakes, lizards and tuatara, their extinct relatives, and some of the extinct ancestors of mammals. Due to their evolutionary history and the diversity of extinct forms, the validity of the class is not universally supported in scientific circles, though in practice, it remains in use by some biologists and more laymen, especially in mass media. The study of reptiles, historically combined with that of amphibians, is called herpetology.

Scientific Classification

Kingdom: Animalia

Phylum: Chordata

Class: Reptilia

Metabolism

Modern reptiles exhibit some form of cold-bloodiness so that they have limited physiological means of keeping the body temperature constant. They often rely on external sources of heat. The benefit of a low resting metabolism is that it requires far less fuel to sustain bodily functions. By using temperature variations in their surroundings, or by remaining cold when they do not need to move, reptiles can save considerable amounts of energy compared to endothermic animals of the same size.

A crocodile needs from a tenth to a fifth of the food necessary for a lion of the same weight and can live a half a year without eating. Lower food requirements and adaptive metabolism sallow reptiles to dominate the animal life in regions where net calorie availability is too low to sustain large-bodied mammals and Birds.

Intelligence

Reptiles are generally considered less intelligent than mammals and birds. The size of their brain relative to their body is much less than that of mammals.

Vision

Most reptiles are diurnal animals. The vision is typically adapted to daytime conditions, with color vision and more advanced visual depth perception than in amphibians and most mammals. In some species, such as blind snakes, vision is reduced. Some snakes have extra sets of visual organs in the forms of pits sensitive to infrared radiation (heat). Such heat-sensitive pits are particularly well developed in the pit vipers, but are also found in Boa's and Pythons. These pits allow the snakes to sense the body heat of birds and mammals, enabling pit vipers to hunt rodents in the dark.

Florida Snakes

There were many more pages of information about reptiles but I decided to research some information about Florida reptiles, focusing on Florida snakes and alligators. I googled 'Florida snakes' and came across a great website which had some very interesting information about them and about snakes in general. I decided to break all the information down to a list of facts.

1. There are 45 different specie of snakes, 6 of which are venomous. The six that are venomous are the Eastern Diamondback rattlesnake, Pygmy rattlesnake, Timber rattlesnake, Copperhead, Coral snake, and the Cottonmouth (water moccasin).

2. You can also find non-native specie of snakes in Florida, as some negligent Pet owners have dumped their pet Pythons into the Everglades when they decided they could not care for them any longer. Unfortunately, those snakes are creating

havoc for other species in the sensitive ecosystems of South Florida. Biologists now estimate that more than 100,000 Pythons and Boa Constrictors live in the Everglades and they are eating all of the native wildlife that do belong there.

3. Snakes are natural predators, feeding on rodents, frogs, invertebrates, birds, and other reptiles. Some snakes are cannibals and will eat other snakes.

4. Snakes play an important role in Florida ecosystems by controlling the population of other animals. This is good for both ecosystems and humans, as the rat and mice populations are regulated by snake predation.

5. All snakes are carnivorous.

6. Some snakes lay eggs, while other give live birth, a process that occurs when the eggs hatch inside the female snake. Mating season for all snakes is in the spring, and the young snakes are born from August until the end of October.

7. Snakes don't have eyelids or ears, and their eyes do not move. To hear they feel vibrations through the ground.

8. They shed their skin 3-4 times a year. This is called molting.

9. Snakes don't smell with their noses. They have a forked or split tongue that they can use to smell and taste chemical compositions in the air. This is called the Jacobson's Organ and is located on the roof of the snakes mouth.

10. Snakes are a vital part of the food chain because not only do they control the rodent population, they are also prey for other animals such as Owls, Hawks, Herons and Alligators.

I knew I had to be on top of my game working with reptiles so I ended my homework session for the evening to go to bed. On top of that, Luna kitty was begging for some attention-how could I possibly resist her playful antics of jumping up and down and running around like a spaz? We played until we were both tuckered out, she fell asleep curled up next to me on my comforter. A few minutes later I joined her in La-La Land. I didn't wake up until it was time for some more learning at the Ranger Academy.

30: Ranger Reptile Training

By the end of the first week of reptile ranger training I realized I don't really love working with reptiles. I mean, they are interesting but really, they don't do much and I find it boring working with them. Having said that, Wildlife Ranger Sheri made perfect sense when she told us that if you live in Florida, you will undoubtedly come across reptiles of all kinds, so you'd better get to know what your encountering when you do. I especially paid attention to the venomous snakes, watching them through the glass windows of their habitat in the Reptile House. As Sheri said, we would never actually work with the dangerous snakes, we would never feed them or clean out their habitats-that was up to the senior Wildlife Rangers only. (And I was very o.k. with that!) The five venomous snake habitats in the back of the Reptile House were labeled "**HOT**" and "**WARNING: VENOMOUS SNAKES DO NOT OPEN**" and they were locked up tight with padlocks. You didn't have to tell me twice.

I was currently in the Wildlife Building kitchen with Drew and Serafina gathering food to feed the non-venomous snakes, which consisted of frozen dead mice of all sizes. Lovely, right? Best part was, (and I'm being sarcastic) we had to thaw the dead rodents out by putting them in warm water. After that we dried them with a blow dryer on the warm setting because snakes like to eat warm food. I also had to thaw out the dead baby mice called "pinkies" to feed the baby snakes. Ugh times 1,000! I resigned myself to the fact that this is just what they eat and that's that. Also, seeing the utter dismay and disgust all over Serafina's face was almost worth it. It made me feel so much better that I was handling it pretty well considering. Drew of course had no problem with the snakes diet, he was actually fascinated by the reptiles in his charge.

"No puedo!" Serafina dramatically exclaimed. "I can't do this! It's just so gross I swear I'll throw up if I continue!!! Drew, will you please do this for me?" She batted her long, dark lashes simultaneously with a huge 150 watt smile. Seeing that made *me* almost want to throw up. I mean, *really*??? Does that work for her?

"No problem Serafina, I'll do your diets. You can go sit down in the Wildlife Lounge until Rayne and I finish."

There was my answer. It definitely works. I sighed and got back to the unpleasant task at hand.

"What's on your mind, Rayne?" Drew asked.

"I'm thinking I'm glad I only have to do this for a short while. I'm also thinking I'll skip lunch today." He laughed when I said that.

"I admire you doing this even though I can tell you don't like it. Your tenacious and determined. Serafina wimped out and to tell you the truth, I only told her I'd do her work so I didn't have to hear her complain anymore." He rolled his eyes and it was my turn to laugh.

We finished sorting out the mice diets and started doling out the food. With some snakes it was easy, you just had to unlock the food slots located on the back door of their habitats and toss the mice in with long handled tongs, and they would eat. Other snakes were finicky though, and needed extra incentives to eat...they wanted to chase and conquer their food. In other words, you had to pick up the dead, thawed out, and warmed up mouse by their tail with the tongs, open up the slot, then dangle it up and down and all around until the snake would lunge at it and grab it with their mouth and teeth. Yes, most snakes have teeth. I also learned that venomous snakes have teeth AND fangs. The fangs are where the venom comes out. Some of the snakes we fed liked to curl up around the mouse and then swallow it. The only good thing about feeding the snakes was the fact that you only had to feed them twice a month, because of their slow metabolism. Drew and I did all the feeding together, Serafina did not participate. Sheri the Wildlife Ranger helped us feed the first couple of snakes then left us to finish feeding the rest. Sheri also taught us how to handle the snakes, weigh them, and pick them up with a snake handle. I learned that some snakes were really mellow, while others were quick as lightning and had to be held with a firm hand. My favorite snake was the Indigo Snake, a highly endangered and rare specie of snake that was incredibly beautiful and so chill. It also was known to eat other venomous snakes, as it was immune to the venom. The one at the Reptile House was four and a half feet long and had shiny, iridescent bluish purple scales. It was quite the handsome snake indeed. Today I fed it a large sized rat, it devoured it quickly. The snake could unhinge its mouth wide enough to engulf the entire rat, then swallow it whole. Come to think about it that snake and Serafina had a lot in common. They were both beautiful, cold blooded, and cunning.

"That's it, that's the last snake to feed, we are done. Just in time for lunch. Would you like to join me for a bite at the Wildlife Cafe?" Drew asked. This time I declined the offer "I'm really not very hungry, and I have to catch up on journaling some new updated information about Yuma. He's going to be transferred to his brand new habitat soon. I'm psyched about that. But thanks for the invite. Next time."

Drew looked disappointed but didn't push. As I left the Reptile House I decided that I was in desperate need of some fresh air on the river after work was over. I was feeling the need to go kayaking on the water to clear my mind and do some exploring. The end of my day could not come fast enough.

31: Blue Waters Cure the Blues

A few hours later I let Beth know I was going kayaking (and after promising to stay very close to home, wear a life jacket, carry my phone in my waterproof case, and wear my marine whistle given to me by Maverick!) I finally found myself on the Blue Spring waters of the Homosassa River. I slowly began to relax with every stroke of my paddle that propelled my kayak forward through the sparkling clear water. The still warm sun combined with the cool wind hitting my face as I glided through the river made me appreciate the reality of my new life, the one my mother planned for me prior to her death. I was feeling melancholy about my mother's death, my heart was hanging on tenaciously to that deeply imbedded sorrow. I found that being among nature was the best medication for my still broken heart. This time on the water was my time, but it also included my mother and father. I thought about and talked to them constantly in my head as I navigated the waterways. All of my senses were magnified on the water, my vision sharper, my sense of smell more intense, my hearing better, my thoughts more clear. This was my form of meditation, I not only had my Mother to thank but Mother Nature as well. I decided to explore some coves off the river to see what I could discover. The homes along the river's banks were always fun to look at, most were very expensive looking. Occasionally I'd see a charming, Florida style cracker house

or cottage that just seemed incredibly romantic to me. I sometimes imagined myself living in one, happily married with children. One day, but not
anytime soon. I have to first live life alone and just do me, especially since
I have discovered what I want to do with my life. The day we rescued Rose
the manatee my fate was sealed~the fire lit that day was now burning even
more brightly within my soul. I was so engrossed with my thoughts I hadn't
noticed the pod of silvery grey dolphins until they practically jumped over
my kayak! They were twirling and flipping in and out of the water playfully
with each other and they seemed to be trying to include me in their water
shenanigans~at least I hoped so! I followed them down a narrow water-
way delighted to take part in their joyful engagement. When I got closer I
grabbed my phone to try and get some good pictures of them. The sun was
going down so I decided to take them quickly, I sure didn't want to kayak
home in the dark. As I was taking the pictures I noticed some movement
in the water next to a big boat docked by a big house nearby. Curious now,
I moved my phone down to take a look. What I saw alarmed me instantly,
even if I didn't know why. It was a man in the water by the boat carrying
something in his hands....and I had his full attention. What in the world
could he be doing in the water this late in the day??? Even though we were
a good distance apart I could clearly see the look of anger flash from his
eyes-it's hard to explain how I knew he was bad news but immediately and
innately I did. My body tensed up as a silent alarm went off in my head,
warning me to turn around and get the heck out of there. I trusted my
intuition and got the heck out of there. I turned my kayak around, paddling
furiously away from the man in the water. I breathed a sigh of relief when I
finally reached the main entry to the river, but I didn't stop until I reached
my dock near the park. It was almost completely dark when I docked the
kayak so I ran home, I didn't want my new family members to worry about
me. As soon as I saw the house I now called home I started to feel safe and
secure and my heart rate slowed down to normal. I decided it was probably
just a randomly weird experience I encountered on the river, but whatever
it was I wanted no part of it. I went inside, and for the rest of the weekend

I tried to forget anything odd had happened on the river. Little did I know then that it was about to get not only more weird, but dangerous too.

32: Ranger Danger

For the next couple of nights I kept dreaming of a giant snake in the water trying to eat me. I would try to swim away from it, only I was swimming in slow motion while it was coming at me from behind with its mouth wide open. Just when it was about to grab me with its fangs I woke up in a cold sweat. I would be glad when this last week of reptile training ended.

"Good Morning Rayne Lanecastor." I heard Drew's now familiar voice behind me.

"Good morning Drew. How are you?"

"Doing great, mate! I just saw Maverick and he told me that there is a meeting today for all Jr. Rangers at noon at the mess hall."

"O.K. then I guess we should get started with our duties, right? I don't see Serafina so she can join us once she gets here. We get the fun job of cleaning up the mess the snakes made after digesting their meals." I grimaced as I said that.

We worked for the next 3 hours straight cleaning reptile habitats. Big surprise, Serafina never showed up. No surprise, I liked it much better that way. When we finished it was time for the meeting, so we locked up the Reptile House then headed to the Wildlife Building . Along the way we ran into Maverick, Mallory, and Jenzy. I told them about the weird encounter I had when I saw the man in the water last Friday.

Mallory summed it up perfectly. "How freaking scary! Mysterious too!"

"I know, I barely slept the last couple of nights thinking about it. I just got spooked, that's all."

"You know, Rayne, there has been a few cases involving the theft of expensive boat parts around Homosassa and Crystal River." Maverick said. "I heard my mom talking about it with one of her friends whose boat motor was stolen recently while she was out of town. Apparently the thieves wait till the homeowners are away then they go to the water and strip the boats to sell them on the black market. In Florida its a huge racket. I'm glad you left right away, maybe you should only go kayaking for a while with a friend, just to be safe. The thieves are most likely local because they know their way around the river. They also know when the homeowners aren't home."

"Maverick is right, Rayne." Mallory added. "Better to be safe than sorry, right?"

I agreed and then we went into the meeting. Ms. Greene was waiting for us.

"I don't want to keep you long since it's lunch time and I know you all are hungry, so I'll be brief. I have received some disturbing reports about a manatee we released last year named CC, the news isn't good. CC has become entangled in a crab trap, the reports say one of his flippers is severely damaged. If he isn't rescued soon, he will most likely die. I'm asking all of you to keep a look out for him, when you are out on the water around the park. Time is of the essence. Any questions?"

"Who do we call if we see him?" Josie asked.

"Call me on my cell phone please." Ms. Greene answered. "If any of you don't have it I'll give it to you. Thank you. Rayne and Drew, Serafina called me this morning saying she was sick, that's why she wasn't there this morning. I meant to come see you both to tell you, then I got the call about CC and I forgot. I'm sorry."

"It's all right Ms. Greene, we got everything done and we only have to clean the back of the Reptile House after lunch." I didn't add that Serafina's absence was just fine with me.

My Uncle Bart came into the Wildlife Building to tell me Beth made us a nice lunch if I'd like to go home and eat. As we were driving by the Reptile House to go home I saw Serafina quickly leaving the Reptile House. I thought that was odd but maybe she was there looking for me or Drew. I waved at her but her head was down so she didn't see me. Something was off about her, not sure what but it did make me curious. I could ask her later what she was doing at the Reptile House when she had already called off but for now I needed some tasty food fuel my Aunt Beth was graciously offering.

My uncle dropped me off at the Reptile House after lunch. Drew wasn't there yet so I unlocked the back door of the Reptile House to let myself in. I didn't even take a few steps inside when I saw it-a brightly colored snake coiled up on the floor just a few steps away from me. Worse than that, it was red, yellow, and black, with the red touching yellow. My cousin Aiden's previous words came to my mind; red touch black, friend of Jack. Red touch yellow, kill a fellow... I was standing face-to-face with a venomous Coral snake, a very beautiful but deadly snake. It was so shocking I was at a total loss of what to do. There comes a time in your life I suppose, when you are faced with a sink or swim situation. I decided that I'm a swimmer and could handle this. But first, I had to calm my nerves. Easier said than done. My heart was beating so quickly I had to take a few deep breaths to slow it down. Besides, the snake was just staring at me and not moving, so that was a plus, right? I looked around the room to see what I could do to contain the snake without hurting it or myself. I noticed there was a tall Rubbermaid bin a few feet behind me so I slowly backed up to it to grab it and gently take the lid off, tucking it under my arm. I also grabbed a snake hook from the wall. I was slowly walking back toward the snake when Drew came barreling in.

"I'm sorry I'm late Rayne!" He said as he came this close to stepping right up to the snake!

"*STOP*!" I said firmly. He stopped immediately, his eyes wide open in disbelief when he saw what he almost stepped on.

"Drew stay where you are-don't move a muscle." I cautioned. I proceeded to calmly walk toward the snake, all the while mentally communicating with it, '*I will not hurt you I am your friend!*' until I was close enough to scoop up the snake with the long snake hook and gently put it into the bin while simultaneously placing the lid over it, effectively trapping the snake inside. I kid you not, a sweat broke out on the scalp of my head I was *that* nervous. When I realized we were safe I exhaled a huge sigh of relief. To my utter astonishment I also did something I never expected and could not control, I started to shake uncontrollably. Drew noticed. He pulled me into his arms telling me it was safe now, that I was brave and that I handled the situation like a pro. Then he called Sheri and Ms. Greene on the radio and asked them to come to the Reptile House ASAP. They were there in five minutes which gave me enough time to collect my wits and compose myself. Drew's warm embrace made me finally stop shaking. I thanked Drew for comforting me.

"Rayne it's you I need to thank. If it wasn't for you I would have stepped right on that snake. You're very brave, what you did was remarkable. I'm impressed."

We watched as Sheri put the Coral Snake back into its habitat, which had been left unlocked and slightly open. That is how it escaped. Sheri asked us if we ever went near the venomous snake habitat section, we told her no. It was very puzzling and disconcerting knowing that a door was left ajar and not locked. They were going to have to investigate all rangers and volunteers to try and find out who was responsible for being so careless. Ms. Greene let us go home for the rest of the day, Drew was sweet and walked me home. After talking to my uncle and aunt about what happened, and after thanking sweet Aiden for the knowledge he gave me about how to identify the snake in the first place, I went up to my comfortable room, jumped on my bed, and crashed hard. Only this time I didn't have any dreams at all, I slept like a rock.

33: Brutus & Bitty

I finished my last week of reptile training with a new found respect and admiration for all things reptile. I was reading in my room when I heard some loud knocking on my door and an extremely excited sounding Aiden saying my name "Rayne! Rayne! Rayne! You must come downstairs right now!! You won't believe what dad brought home!" With that exclamation I heard him run down the stairs just as fast as he came up. I hurried downstairs, when I reached the living room I could barely believe what I was seeing, because I'd swear I was looking at two very tiny and very adorable baby black bears. Bears! Was I looking at baby BEARS??? I blinked my eyes a couple of times, and I heard Uncle Bart chuckle.

"Yes Rayne, I've brought home two baby black bears that were found abandoned by their mother in the Ocala National Forest. Their mother has been tagged and was tracked going in the opposite direction. We have been asked to raise them, and to give them a new home here at the Wildlife Park. Beth and I are going to take the first couple of days and nights with them and then the wildlife mammal staff will care for them. For the next three months they will be bottle fed a diet of mammal milk replacer every four hours, and it's time to feed them now. Come closer and watch."

"Awesome!" I quickly replied.

"Beth and I will show you and Aiden how to properly hold them while bottle feeding them then let you guys take a turn. They are small and weak now, but as they get bigger and stronger it will take some getting use to. Mainly because they are just naturally strong and have claws. It's pretty easy to feed them now." Uncle Bart picked up one of the cubs and Aunt Beth picked up the other, and oh my goodness they were just the cutest little black balls of fluff I had ever laid eyes on. They had tiny and shiny black button eyes and a soft looking little brown nose. Aiden and I watched them guzzle down the milk from the bottle while making cute little grunts and smacks. When they were finished drinking the milk we all spent the next hour watching them roll around and play with each other until they got tuckered out. Once again I found it incredible that this was my new life, living in Florida and playing with baby bears.

"What are their names, dad?" Aiden asked.

"The Biologists that found them called this one Brutus, because he's a boy and big, and they called her Bitty because she's tiny. It's time for them to nap now, but if you two would like we will let you both feed them four hours from now." He said to us as he put them in a huge pet carrier with a soft rug in it for them to lay on.

"Yes please!" Aiden and I said in unison. We looked at each other and we all laughed.

"Well then since that's settled come in the kitchen with me and I'll make some sandwiches. Aunt Beth said. "But please go wash your hands first?"

After eating I excused myself to go upstairs and do some research on Florida Black Bears. I got my iPad out and started the search.

Florida Black Bear

Scientific Classification

Kingdom: Animalia

Phylum: Chordata

Class: Mammalia

Order: Carnivora

Family: Ursidae

Genus: Ursus

Species: U.americanus

The Florida Black Bear (Urses americanus floridanus) is a subspecies of the American black bear that has historically ranged throughout most of Florida and southern portions of Alabama, Georgia, and Mississippi. The large black-furred bears live mainly in forested areas and have seen recent habitat reduction throughout the state.

Florida black bears are typically large-bodied with shiny black fur, a light brown nose, and a short stubby tail. A white chest patch is also common on many but not all the bears. It is currently Florida›s largest terrestrial mammal with an average male weight of 300 pounds and a few have grown to 500 ponds. Females generally weigh less and on average are about 198 pounds. Average adults have a length of between 4 feet and 6 feet and they also stand between 2.5 feet and 3.5 feet high at the shoulder.

Florida black bears are mainly solitary, except when in groups or pairings during mating season. Although they are solitary mammals, in general, most are not territorial, and typically do not defend their range from other bears. Black bears have good eyesight, acute hearing, and an excellent sense of smell.

CONSERVATION

Habitat loss is greatly affecting Florida black bear populations. Nearly 20 acres of wildlife habitat are lost to new development every hour in Florida. Bears being injured or killed by motorists are another threat to regional populations. Since 1976 there have been more than 1,356 documented cases of bears being killed in Florida. Over 100 bears are killed on Florida roadways each year, and in 2002 a record 132 deaths occurred. That makes roadkill the number one cause of Bear death in the state.

Bear sightings have been in increasing in Florida in recent years and the Florida Fish and Wildlife Conservation Center has posted a number of actions that can be taken to discourage bears from encroaching into human occupied areas. Most importantly, don't allow access to food sources. Keep garbage cans in the garage or put locks on the lids. Don't keep pet foods outdoors and don't use feeders. Clean outdoor grills, and motion activated alarms are an effective way to scare bears away.

I printed up my new information sheet on Florida Black Bears and added it to my wildlife folder. I really felt like I was learning so much about Florida wildlife and I couldn›t find it more interesting! I wanted to give my brain a rest so I put my iPad away and sent a picture text to Mallory.

> *Mallory! Guess what?*
>
> *Hey Rayne!!! What's up doll????*
>
> *Baby Bear Cubs!!*
>
> *My mom told me! Maverick & I want to come over!!!!*
>
> *Cool, come over! See you soon!*

I went downstairs to see if it was ok for them to come over (since I already invited them) and my Aunt said of course it was, especially since Maverick would most likely be helping with their feeding schedule. She said he's been doing an excellent job raising Yuma who was growing steadily and becoming very healthy. I told her I could tell that Yuma was doing good because I was recording his progress and his appetite increased every day. The only downside I thought to myself was that I hardly see Maverick since he started his care of Yuma. I ran back upstairs to brush my hair and put on just a hint of perfume I got from my mom last Christmas. Right when I finished I heard a knock on my door.

"Come in!" I said. Mallory walked in and Maverick was right behind her. Mallory came running to me pulling me into a bear hug.

"Raaaayne!!!! My new best friendddddddd!" She drawled then let me go. "Maverick did I not tell you how lit her room is? I love it so much!" She looked his way and he nodded his head yes.

My eyes met his and I'd swear I could feel a bolt of electricity surge through my body. *What in the heck???*

"Your room is dope, Rayne." He walked over to the picture of me and my parents. "May I?" He asked if he could pick it up.

"Yes of course. I'd like it very much if you and Mallory made yourselves comfortable. That's my parents."

He looked intently at the picture, then put it gingerly back in its place.

"You look like both of them. Your mother was very beautiful and your dad is beaming."

Maverick's words touched me. I thanked him.

I offered them a soda and we sat down in the living room. We talked about the bears for a little bit then Maverick asked me about the snake incident in the Reptile House the day before.

I told them what happened, and when I got to the part about Drew helping me calm down, I could see Mavericks eyes turn dark and he seemed annoyed. Could he be jealous?

"I'm so mad your life was put in jeopardy." He fumed.

Oh. I thought. Not jealous, but concerned for my safety. Bummer and great at the same time.

"I heard you handled it like an experienced Reptile Ranger. How on earth did you not freak out?" Mallory's eyes were wide with curiosity.

"I'm not exactly sure, Mallory." I laughed. "I just gathered my wits, formed a game plan, and proceeded cautiously. "You would have done the same thing?"

"No she would have screamed and jumped in Drew's arms!" Maverick teased his twin, and Mallory giggled.

"He's absolutely right! In fact Drew praised you so much I admit I'm a little jelly!" She pouted.

Again I saw a flash of annoyance in Mavericks eyes. **#YAY!**

"Well there's no reason whatsoever to be jelly Mallory, I think Drew was just happy I stopped him from stepping near the Coral snake, that's all."

"It's a blessing Serafina was sick and not there." Maverick said.

Great. Now I felt annoyed. He cared about Serafina.

"Only because she would have been a hot mess." He added.

That made me feel better, I think. Unlike Florida Black Bears I was finding out that I'm definitely territorial when it comes to Maverick Greene.

"You know the weird thing about Serafina is that I saw her leaving the Reptile House in a hurry after our staff meeting-and that was before I found the escaped snake. I wonder if she saw anything unusual? I couldn't ask her because she never came back that day. I'll ask her when I see her on Monday."

"That is weird." Mallory mused. "If she was sick why was she there at all? Seems fishy to me."

I hadn't noticed until now that Luna my cat had meandered her way onto Mavericks lap, and was purring contentedly while he rubbed her head and back. Apparently all females-even the furry kind- were not immune to his charms. I grabbed my phone so I could take their picture, asking him if that was ok.

"Sure if you want." He said and smiled. "She's a great cat."

"Thanks Maverick I adore her." I took the picture. And just like Luna, I was a smitten kitten. He likes my cat. **#YayAgain!!**

I went to my photo's to see how the picture came out, it did not disappoint. The photo's behind it were photos of the wild dolphin pod I had seen on the water last week so I decided to show them to Maverick and Mallory. As we swiped through the pictures the one of the man in the water came up. I instantly felt uneasy when I saw it. "Look guys, that's the man I saw in the water that startled me!"

"That's so creepy!" Mallory squealed.

"I know, right?" I added.

"You know, you may have something here." Maverick said. "Look to the right of him. Do you see the small boat in the background?" He expanded the picture to a bigger size and then I did see it. It was a grey boat with an orange stripe down the middle, it was the same boat that almost hit the manatees that day Maverick and I were kayaking.

"I recognize that boat Maverick! And look!" I pointed to another image, and near that boat was another man.

"I see him." Maverick got really serious then. "That boat belongs to the Hick brothers, and that means nothing good. Do me a favor Rayne, don't go out kayaking or paddle boarding by yourself anymore. Promise me."

"I don't think it's any big deal but I promise."

"Well now since that's settled I'd love to see the bear cubs!" Mallory declared.

"Ok, let's go, but I warn you Mallory, you are going to fall in love!"

We went downstairs to see the baby bears and just like I said Mallory fell completely in love with them. Who wouldn't? After they left we ate dinner and watched movies together, like a family. It was nice. I was beginning to feel like I completely belonged here. **#ThanksMom**

34: Education Station

Jenzy and I checked the weekly training schedule on the Jr. Ranger bulletin board in the Wildlife building to see where we would train next. To our immense delight we saw that we were going to learn how to perform Interpretive Educational programs. Under the heading Interpretive & Educational Programs were four names, Jenzy, Josephine, Mallory, and Rayne. The only thing keeping me from being totally psyched about this was seeing the two names under the heading Manatee Training: Maverick and Serafina. I knew that would eventually happen but it still kind of felt like a kick to the gut to actually see it. Thankfully Josie and Mallory showed up just then to pull me out of that little funk. Mallory squealed in delight and high fived Josie then we all headed to the Education building, which was located near the entrance of the park. Aunt Beth had an office in the building and there was also a study room, small kitchen, a library called the Florida room, a few more staff offices and storage rooms. We all went to the study room where my Aunt Beth was waiting for us.

"Sit down girls, please get comfortable. We are going to be here all week long, I have so much to teach you! I'm passionate about Education, by the end of the week I hope you will be too!" She beamed a big smile our way then began.

"Welcome Jr. Rangers to Education week. I believe Education is one of the very most important aspects of wildlife preservation. If we can educate people, especially children, about wildlife and the problems they face in the environment, or if they get to know the wildlife they are looking at, then they will care and do something to help. Every environmental and wildlife organization has an Education Director and some type of Environmental Interpretation program, so that the public will know just exactly what they stand for or are trying to accomplish. These are the three most important keys to becoming an effective Educator:

1. Know your facts.

2. Memorize what you want to say.

3. Engage your audience

If you accomplish and get comfortable with those three things you will see that combined with your passion, you will get the job done of educating the public. If you are shy about speaking publicly in front of an audience, you will find that knowing what you want to say and practicing saying it will give you the confidence to do it. Another great tool in educating the public about your environmental organization is the use of social media. Using social media is free, and reaches large audiences. This week each of you have to pick a subject you are passionate about and at the end of the week you have to do a presentation educating us about it. Be creative, think outside the box. Spend the rest of the mornings this week looking over our educational tools here at the park and studying in our study room, breaking for lunch at noon. Please attend the Interpretive programs here at the park so you can learn our approach to Educating the guests who come to our park. If you have any questions my office is right down the hall. Finally, you will be required to go to the Manatee Festival in Crystal River which is coming up soon. You will learn firsthand what it's like to do Outreach programs. Please study up on the wildlife here at the park and be prepared for that. Until then happy studying! With that she left and we all got to work. Another week of learning and it was time for a fun event. Manatee Festival here I come!

35: Manatee Festival

"**H**ey Rayne, we're almost there!" Josie said with excitement. "Manatee Festival fun ahead!"

I snapped out of my deep thoughts regarding my upcoming Educational Presentation I had to do tomorrow. I spent the last couple of days studying and watching all of the Interpretive programs at the park, and I decided to do my presentation about the use of Social Media to promote your environmental organization. I was finished with my research and had it all formatted. Now I was just trying to mentally prepare myself for the actual presentation taking place in front of others. Nothing to it but to do it, I thought. Meanwhile, Josie and I were selected to work the morning shift at a booth the Wildlife Department had at the Crystal River Manatee Festival, a four day street festival that Crystal River has every year. Mallory and Jenzy were working the afternoon shift, and Josie and I decided we would walk around the festival after they came to relieve us. I was looking forward to seeing what a Manatee Festival was all about, I brought some money for food and other items for sale. I wanted to buy some kind of thank you gifts for my new family, because they have been so welcoming, making me feel a part of the family from the very beginning. I will always be appreciative of that. We found our booth located in an area where there were other non-for-profit organizations. Sheri from the

Wildlife Department was putting out terrariums on the table. She greeted us warmly with her megawatt smile.

"Hi Girls, welcome to the Manatee Festival! Our job today is to promote the Wildlife Park. We have these pamphlets to hand out that has information about the park, and these terrariums to show visitors, one with a previously injured Box turtle being rehabbed and another with a Red Rat snake to educate the public about the importance of snakes in Florida's environment. Maverick will be bringing a Great Horned Owl here soon that is permanently injured due to an unfortunate encounter with a car windshield. Just be yourselves and engage as many people as you can. Any questions?"

Josie and I both shook our heads no and Sheri spent the next five minutes telling us more about the two reptiles. I was trying so hard to pay attention but my mind kept drifting back to the 'Maverick was on his way' here part. That boy definitely has an effect on my central nervous system! I also noticed my good mood just got even better. Thirty minutes later Maverick did show up but Josie and I were deep in conversations with visitors so I only had a chance to say hi and smile with a wave. He smiled back with a wink. Josie noticed the exchange, giving me a raised eyebrow inquisitive look, her soulful brown eyes filled with curiosity. I just smiled at her and kept talking, and the next couple of hours just flew by. The Festival was packed and our booth was very popular. I found that people loved hearing about the Wildlife Park, plus the animals were a huge attraction. Watching Maverick holding the Great Horned Owl on his arm while animatedly talking about it made me like him even more, if that was possible. You could tell that he was genuinely passionate about the very cool Owl, and he was surrounded by visitors, many of which were girls our age. The girls were looking at him like I imagined I looked when watching him~with major appreciation.

"He's very handsome." Josie said from behind me.

"That he is, Josie." I replied.

"You like him, don't you?"

I turned around and faced her. "Is it that obvious?"

"Maybe not to others, but I'm very observant. Just so you know, it's more obvious that he likes you. He keeps staring over here looking for you."

"Really? Like for real, real?" I sounded like an idiot.

"For real, real." She laughed.

"Well thanks for saying that, though I'm not entirely sure that's true. He's so popular and even Serafina likes him-he could have any girlfriend he wants. Why on earth would he want me?" I wondered out loud.

"You're naturally pretty without trying, and you are kind. You also have this inner light within you that makes you shine on the outside. You are genuine. You are also a bit mysterious and that is intriguing. You make people feel comfortable when you're around them. I liked you immediately, and that *never* happens." She laughed again.

"Josie, thank you. That's quite possibly the nicest thing that any one has ever said to me. And for the record, I liked you immediately too." I grabbed her into a hug. She hugged me back and then we went back to work. We didn't stop until Mallory and Jenzy showed up to take our places. It was time for Josie and I to explore the Festival, so we said our goodbyes and off we went.

36: Festival Fun Interrupted by One

Josie and I spent the rest of the afternoon eating and shopping, then eating some more. We ate frozen Key Lime pie covered with chocolate on a stick, funnel cakes, and we even ate something healthy, we shared a blackened Grouper sandwich that was so delicious it practically melted in your mouth while simultaneously waking up your taste buds with a spicy yet buttery kick. Florida cuisine is the bomb, for sure. When we shopped I found some great homemade gifts for my new family. For Bart I got a hand carved wooden Black Bear Christmas tree ornament, for Beth I bought homemade bottled vanilla extract and a jar of locally harvested wildflower honey, and for the darling Aiden I bought a very colorful hand painted and exquisitely made kite in the shape of a Macaw Parrot. For myself I bought the most aromatic homemade soap called Lavender Dreams. In fact I was so engrossed in homemade soap smelling that I lost Josie for a minute, she had wondered off to another booth so I paid the vendor and hurried after her. I was looking around for her when someone from behind me pushed me so forcibly hard my purchases went flying and so did I. I stumbled, then fell face first on to the unyielding ground. I was now in a planking position practically eating dirt, it wasn't pleasant, it really hurt. **#Ouch!** *What the Heck?!?!?* I laid on the ground for a moment to catch my breath wondering what, or who, had hit me so hard. I turned my body around to look and what I saw made my blood turn cold. My 'female intuition' totally kicked in once again but this time it wasn't good. Looming over me was a guy wearing a camouflage baseball hat and dark sunglasses. I couldn't see his eyes but I could tell by the tight line of his mouth that he was as mean as a viper snake and NOT a happy camper.

"You need to be careful there young lady! Let me help you up." He reached down and grabbed my arm, squeezing it painfully hard while yanking me up. That's when he hissed at me a warning: "You better watch your back little lady, or you're gonna get hurt real bad."

I tried to call out but instead I winced in pain. Before I managed to pull my arm away from his vice grip I noticed he had a very large and ugly tattoo on his arm. The tattoo was of a revolver that had a rebel flag coming out of it. He noticed my staring at it so he let go of me quickly then disappeared into the crowd. I stood there completely stunned in disbelief, wondering if it was my imagination or was that a sincere threat? And why on earth was that guy making threats to me? I was still shaking and on the verge of crying when Josie came up to me.

"Look what I bought, Rayne!" She held up a glass beaded necklace.

"It's very pretty, Josie." As I said that I realized my voice was a shaky whisper.

"What's wrong, Rayne?" She immediately put the necklace down. "You look like you've seen a ghost, you're so pale!" She said with alarmed concern.

"Not a ghost, Josie, I just had an encounter with a very bad guy, and I think I know who he is. Do you mind if we go back to the booth and then home? I need to talk to my Uncle Bart, I have to check something out."

"Absolutely Rayne." Then she did something only a good and caring friend would do, she entwined her arm with mine and guided me there. #FriendsForever

37: Home Safe Home

When Josie and I got back to the booth I told Maverick and the girls what happened to me. Maverick gallantly took over, insisting on driving me home. I called my Uncle Bart to tell him I needed to talk to him and Aunt Beth when we got there. He assured me they would be waiting. I checked my phone to take a better look at the pictures I had taken that day I followed the dolphins into the cove with the nice house on the water.

"Rayne, the Hicks brothers are extremely dangerous, if you have some pictures of them up to no good then it's a big problem. First of all, I'm never letting you out of my sight. Second, we need to show those pictures to the Sheriff. Your uncle is friends with him. He's a good man and undoubtably very familiar with the Hicks family." As Maverick was talking to me I noticed his jaw was clenched and he was gripping the steering wheel tightly.

"I went to middle school with one of the Hicks Brothers, his name is Rod and he is two years older than me but we were in the same grade. He was and probably still is a huge bully, constantly picking fights with any kid who crossed his path. He was held back a few times in school for failing grades and fighting in school. One day, I crossed his path, and it's a day I'll never forget. That day was the first time I ever experienced pure anger,

anger I couldn't control. I was walking home from baseball practice when I heard a wailing yelp of pain. To my complete shock I realized that it was Rod Hicks and he was kicking a dog---repeatedly! He was yelling "*YOU STUPID DOG!*" He was so intent on hurting the dog that he didn't see me coming. That's when I did something I've never done before, I grabbed his arm turning him around to face me and I knocked him flat to the ground.

"Don't you **EVER** hurt an animal **EVER** again-do you hear me?" I yelled at him. "Does it make you feel good to hurt something so defenseless? Get away from here before I do something more I'll regret!"

"Oh no the poor dog! Thank God you were able to stop him!" I put my hand on his shoulder to let him know I was moved by his story, and by him as well.

I was operating on pure adrenaline, Rayne, I had to stop myself from seriously hurting him like he hurt the dog. Rod got up and quickly ran away like the coward he is. I will never forget the look in his eyes as I spun him around though, they were the eyes of a hateful madman who was actually enjoying beating up that defenseless dog. After Rod scurried away I picked up the injured dog that was whimpering in pain, carrying him home to my mom. It's only because she is such a great Veterinarian that the dog lives, he had broken ribs, a broken leg, collapsed lungs, and many more horrible injuries. We nursed him back to health and with a lot of unconditional love he prospered and eventually blossomed into the happy dog he is today. We found him the perfect home with Ranger Sheri, she named him Lucky. Now any time I see Rod Hicks he still can't look at me directly in my eyes, but it's not often I see him anymore, because he dropped out of school in eighth grade."

He finished his story as we pulled into my driveway. I told him what a hero I thought he was for saving Lucky the dog. It made me very sad to know someone could do something so cruel. We went inside where my aunt and uncle were waiting for me and I told them what happened, showing them the finger marks on my arm that were quickly developing into angry bruises. My Uncle Bart called his friend Sheriff Lawsy, who came over a short time later. The Sheriff was a tall man who walked with an air of confident authority and rugged grace. I showed them all the pictures I took that day, then told the Sheriff about being pushed down and threatened. I gave them a description of what the guy looked like, telling them about his tattoo. When the Sheriff saw the finger shaped bruises on my arm he looked to my Uncle Bart.

"Bart, I'll find out who did this I promise." He looked at the pictures I took that night.

"Do you recognize this house?" He showed my uncle.

"Yes. It's the Mayor's house off Pelican Cove."

"That's what I thought. I don't think it's a coincidence that they just got their very expensive boat stripped of boat parts recently. Bart, I think it's quite possible Rayne inadvertently witnessed a crime. Rayne, I'm going to need an official statement from you at headquarters, I need you to give a description of the man who assaulted you earlier today. I'd also like you to email those pictures to me. Here is my card with the email address, and my personal number for you to call whenever you need. Please don't ever hesitate to use it, *especially* if you feel threatened or scared." He handed the card to me. "As a safety precaution from here on out, I don't want you going anywhere alone without a chaperone."

My uncle assured him he wouldn't let that happen, telling him that he would bring me in to the station after work tomorrow. He walked the Sheriff to his car, and my Aunt Beth left to go make dinner for us after she hugged me tight. I thanked Maverick before he left for caring and for taking me home. I was completely exhausted and in need of a very long, and very relaxing, bath. After dinner I practiced my presentation as a distraction until I couldn't keep my eyes open any longer. Tomorrow I'd give this craziness more thought, but for now I fell into a gratefully deep and blissful sleep.

38: Education Presentation

Getting myself out of the bed early the next morning was hard, really hard. I wanted to stay in bed all day curled up with my cat Luna. What I wanted even more was a hug from my mother, along with her reassurance that everything was going to be o.k. Knowing I couldn't have that created an ache so deep in my soul it felt like physical pain, but was infinitely more painful. The tears accumulated slowly then erupted, cascading down my face on to my pillow. I couldn't stop the wracking sobs that came next, nor did I want to. I needed this release, had to have it. I muffled my sobs into my pillows because I didn't want to worry anyone, this was my own private misery to be dealt with, not to be shared. I felt like if I could purge this unhappiness from my body in the form of tears I could start to deal with life again, and after about a half hour of being a complete hot mess that's exactly how I felt. With the release of sorrow came peace. It was times like this that I was so happy to have the private notes my mom wrote to me before dying, they consoled me so much. I grabbed my iPad and went to the note app. I looked down the list and came across one that brought back some fond memories. I couldn't wait to see what she wrote, because it was about me.

6th Grade Debate Champion

Dearest Rayne, it was when you were in 6th grade that I realized what a determined and spunky young lady you had become. You joined the Debate Club as an extra curricular activity that year, and you loved it. The teacher was fun and engaging, and you discovered that you enjoyed discussing current events while debating the pros and cons of each issue. I wonder if you remember how hard you studied and practiced for the title of 'Debate Champion' because I sure do. For two weeks you did nothing but research your topic, which was about animals made to perform in Circuses. You and I had countless conversations about that, you ended up being very knowledgeable about this issue because you were very passionately opposed to it. I must have listened to your talking points a hundred times those two weeks! The night before the big debate you came into my bedroom to tell me you didn't think you could do it because you were so nervous about standing in front of your friends as an audience. Your eyes were wide as saucers and your chin was quivering, you didn't like feeling afraid to do something you needed to do. You climbed in my bed and we talked until you fell asleep. The next morning you woke up refreshed and ready for battle. Over breakfast I asked if you were nervous and you said no, that you had a dream where you saw your father, and that he told you that you did your homework, you were well prepared and that you could do anything you set your mind to do. You also said that your dad told you that everybody else in the debate was nervous too, that you were not alone, and that confidence was the key. "Go get 'em, Tiger!" you said he told you in that dream. What you didn't see was that your words knocked the breath out of me and brought me to tears, so much so that I had to pretend to make another cup of coffee to pull myself together. You see, I had heard that phrase before. Your dad always said that exact same thing to me whenever I had needed encouragement! Rayne honey, you didn't realize it then but you had just given me the most amazing gift! You validated my sincere desire to believe your father was always looking over us. With joy cursing through my veins I told you how proud I was and that I'd be sitting in the audience as your biggest supporter and cheerleader and that I believed in you always & forever. Watching you win that debate was one of the proudest moments of my life. You were smart, calm, respectful, confident, even humorous. You owned that stage. Rayne, don't ever forget what a champion you are, and that I'm now with your dad watching over you. "GO GET 'EM, TIGER!"

I finished the note and wondered how it was possible that I could have picked the perfect letter from my mom to me to read for strength, but somehow I found it. I had a big day ahead of me and I had to slay it. Two hours later that's exactly what I did. I made my presentation and everyone loved it. Aunt Beth said my power point presentation on Social Media motivated her to start a Facebook and Instagram page for the park. She also said I would be an excellent Educator in the wildlife world. There was only one thing that kept me from feeling great about the day and that was the thought of what I had to face next. Uncle Bart was picking me up to take me to the police station to make a statement about the disturbing incident at the festival. I didn't know how I had gotten myself involved with this mess, but I had and it totally sucked. I could not wait for this day to be over, and when it was, I was going to hole up in my room with my cat, watch bad T.V. and eat junk food all weekend long.

39: Crystal River Finest

The police station was located in Downtown Crystal River. Sheriff Lawsy greeted us at the front door with a big smile and a handshake for my Uncle Bart. "Hello again, Rayne. Welcome to the Crystal River police station. How about I show you around before we get started?" He asked, with another big smile. He made me feel comfortable and safe.

"I'd like that, Sheriff Lawsy, thank you." I replied. I'd never been inside a police station and this one was pretty nice, not even remotely like the ones I've seen on television. Crystal River is a small town and probably doesn't have a whole lot of bad guy criminals, and of course this wasn't the county jail. I was relieved to see that the station actually resembled a nice business office. The front room was the reception area and then there were more offices, restrooms, and a kitchen in the back. Sheriff Lawsy took us to his office, it was large and had maps of Crystal River on the walls. He asked us to take a seat then began.

"I want to be the one who takes Rayne's statement today, not just because we are friends, Bart, but because I want Rayne to be as comfortable as she can be. I am not happy this young lady has been assaulted in my town, I intend to rectify this situation. Is that O.K. with you Rayne?"

"Yes Sir." I said.

"Thank you Sheriff." My uncle added.

"Alright let's get started. After we are finished taking your verbal statement we will ask you to put it on paper. I'd also like you to look at some photos of men who live in this area with previous records." He added.

For the next hour I told him my story starting with the day I followed the dolphins into the cove, and finishing with the scary encounter at the festival. I also told the Sheriff how I recognized the Hicks Brothers boat, having encountered it previously with Maverick when Kayaking. The whole time I talked the Sheriff wrote notes while recording my words on a tape recorder. When I got to the part about the guy pushing me down then grabbing my arm painfully to 'help me up' the Sheriffs whole demeanor changed. He looked mad and concerned at the same time. I looked over at my Uncle Bart, he did too.

"Can you show me again where he grabbed you, Rayne?" Sheriff Lawsy asked.

I lifted up my long sleeve and showed him the bruises, which were now an angry purple and mottled green color.

"Thank you, Rayne. You can clearly see the finger marks where he grabbed you. With your permission I'd like someone to come in and take a few pictures of your arm."

A friendly female Deputy came in to take the pictures. She also brought with her two huge binders filled with mugshots of men who had previously been arrested. I looked through the pictures taking my time to be accurate. Sheriff Lawsy and my Uncle Bart walked away to talk while I did. A short time later I came across a photo that resembled the guy who threatened me, but I couldn't be sure. This guy might be considered handsome in a bad boy pissed off at the world kind of way- but his eyes betrayed his good looks. They were cold as ice and full of pent up anger. I never saw his eyes at the Manatee Festival that day because of the large and dark sunglasses he was wearing. I put it aside then continued to look, but no other faces looked similar. I showed Sheriff Lawsy the one picture I had picked out. I could tell he knew who it was.

"To be honest Sheriff Lawsy, I'm not sure that is him. He was wearing a camouflage hat and dark glasses. The only thing I know I can identify for sure is the tattoo."

"You did great Rayne. Take a look at this." The Sheriff pulled two photos out of a file lying on his desk.

What I saw made me gasp out loud and tense up at the same time. The first photo was the same mugshot-only this time you could clearly see his arm with the tattoo of the gun with the rebel flag on it. The second one had his mugshot with his name under it. It said **ROD HICKS**. Crap. I thought. That is *not* good.

"I know this young man and his family too. The Hicks family is notorious around town, I have arrested just about every member of that family at one time or another, mostly for public intoxication, but also for assault violations due to bar fights and petty theft violations. The Hicks family have a homestead in old Homosassa and they are the worst kind of trouble. Their neighbors are scared witless of them. Two months ago Rod Hicks and his brother Duane were arrested by the FWC, the Florida Wildlife Commission, for using illegal gill nets. They lied and said they were using them to catch Mullet. What they were really catching though was every fish and animal they could to sell on the black market, like Snook and Redfish, and even turtles and baby alligators. It's against the law, Rayne, to catch certain fish and even Alligators out of season, and especially without the proper permits, which they did not have. The black market is in old Homosassa, we are constantly trying to close it down, but they are very clever and always seem to know when we're coming. The neighbors knew about this, but only confirmed it after we asked them, as you can imagine they were reluctant to do so. Anyway, they were arrested, fined, and then let go on bail until their trial. That is how we obtained these pictures of the Hicks Brothers, these photos are their mugshots. Now we have this other problem. Citrus County has had a string of luxury boat robberies over the past two years, some very expensive boats are being stripped of everything; engines, anchors, GPS systems-even seat cushions and life jackets. I think you inadvertently came across a crime scene in progress that day on the water, Rayne. The pictures you took are of great interest to us, we are going to investigate them and the Hicks Family very closely once more. Those pictures just might be the very clue we have been searching for to help solve these crimes."

I wrote my statement down on paper then my Uncle Bart took me home. I felt like I had stumbled upon a hornets nest and I just didn't want to think about it any more for a couple of days, at least for the weekend. Come Monday I'll deal with it. Until then I was going to enjoy the warmth and security of my new home, I wasn't venturing out anywhere. It was time to pretend I was a hermit crab going deep into my shell, and I could not wait to burrow.

40: Back to Reality

My uncle and aunt seemed to know I needed a quiet and lazy weekend, they let me be and only came up to check on me and offer me food. They reassured me that I was very loved and would always be safe with them. That meant everything to me, I totally believed them. I did manage to venture out once for fresh air with a walk down to the dock with Aiden on Sunday. Aunt Beth thoughtfully packed us a lunch of fruit, cheese & crackers to enjoy while lazily lounging by the water soaking up the sun. The more time spent with Aiden the more I realized how much my heart had fallen in love with his sweet soul, I knew that I would protect him always and be there for him just as any big sister would. I longed to venture out in a kayak but instinctively I knew that it wasn't a good idea to do so. Now it was time to meet the beginning of the week head on...especially since we had only two more weeks of Wildlife Ranger Academy and then fingers crossed, Graduation. If that wasn't enough to keep me focused and busy then I could always think about the Wildlife Ball at the end of Graduation, an event I was immensely excited about. I kept those pleasant thoughts within and on Monday morning I made my way with my Uncle Bart to the Wildlife Building to get my training duties for the week.

"Have a great day Rayne, I'll pick you up at 2 this afternoon to take you home."

"O.K. Uncle Bart, see you then!" I knew he didn't want me walking home alone.

I went to the Bulletin Board and found out that I would be training for a week in the MOO building to work with manatees. I would also be learning about and training to care for the Key Deer which were located near the manatees in a very large habitat exhibit. Key Deer's are tiny deer living only in the Florida Keys that unfortunately are very endangered. I couldn't be happier that I would be learning how to care for them and the very wonderful manatees too. I was psyched to see Mallory would be joining me.

"Hi, Rayne." Maverick in all his magnificent morning glory joined me at the Bulletin Board. Seeing him made my happiness meter spike up to the roof.

"Hello Maverick, good morning. How are you?"

"Better now, Rayne. I thought about you all weekend. It took everything I had not to come to your house to see you. I ran into your aunt at the Wildlife Building and she said you were laying low, so I decided not to bother you, but only because I knew I'd see you today."

I was processing what he said to me when I heard Serafina's slightly obnoxious voice coming closer, she was with Jenzy and Drew. That instantly ended my intimate moment with Maverick. Curses! I thought to myself. She has the most uncanny timing ever!

"Buenos días Maverick!" Her syrupy voice crooned, focusing on him. I obviously was invisible to her. Big surprise. Huge.

"Good morning everyone." He said, *not* focusing on her. **#happydance!**

We made plans to meet for lunch at the Wildlife Cafe, then Mallory and I headed off to the MOO building. I was ready to dig in and focus on learning anything and everything I could about the gentle giants, the manatees. I knew I was so very lucky to have the healing of my heart hastened by the magical world of Wildlife.

"Time for lunch, Doll!"Mallory drawled as she got up from her desk in the Moo building. "We've been studying hard all morning, and I am weak from hunger. I can't wait any longer I must eat!"

"Can't wait to eat or see Drew?" I teased.

"Both!" She admitted with a huge grin.

We ordered our food at the Wildlife Café then joined the others already sitting there, Drew, Mav, Liam, Jenzy, Josephine, and a very glum looking, quiet for a change, Serafina. Drew and Maverick stood up to greet us.

"I saved these seats for you." Maverick said with a smile directly aimed my way. **#awesomesauce!**

We sat down and for the next half hour we ate and laughed, enjoying each other's company with the exception of Serafina, who never once cracked a smile. What is wrong with her? I wondered. I had no clue but it was definitely not like her to not want to be the center of attention. She did perk up once though and that was when Josie asked me how I was doing this morning, after all the craziness that happened at the festival last week.

"I was very worried for you after your scary encounter with that horrible guy Rayne, when I saw your face afterward I just knew something awful had happened to you!" Josephine declared. "I am so mad that he scared you so!"

"Not as mad as me." Maverick said. "That will not happen again if I have anything to do with it." He added.

"I'm fine, thank you both for your concern. It was very unpleasant but it's over now. Maverick, I know as long as your around me I'm completely safe, just like Lucky the dog was after you saved him from that hateful boy that day. I appreciate you, big time."

"My Dad said your Uncle Bart took you to the police station to file a report about the incident." Jenzy said.

I heard a soft yet clearly audible gasp coming from Serafina's direction. I noticed she had definitely snapped out of her funk- her eyes were laser focused on me. I don't know why but instinctively I knew I had to shut down this conversation. I sure wasn't going to tell everyone about the rest of the investigation that was happening now by Sheriff Lawsy.

"Yes, but it was no big deal, Jenzy. I couldn't pick anyone out." I didn't feel good about lying to her, but it was only a temporary lie. I would tell her the truth in private later when I could. Serafina collected her lunch remnants and backpack and said goodbye to us all rather abruptly. Her exact words were: "Adios amigos gotta go" and off she went. I realized that I was the only one who noticed her weird behavior. I was sensing that now familiar feeling called female intuition, something was up with Serafina, and I intended to find out what it was. I felt sure that it had something to do with me. I made a mental note to myself to talk to her later. I had a few questions for her concerning that day I saw her running away from the reptile building when she was supposed to be sick, that day when I had encountered the venomous snake. I wasn't quite sure why, but my instincts had to be acknowledged, so I would talk to her soon.

After lunch Maverick and Drew walked Mallory and I back to the Moo Building. I enjoyed watching Mallory deeply engaged in conversation with her crush. Drew seemed captivated by her bubbly personality, that was a good sign.

"Can I walk you home after work?" Maverick asked me.

"My Uncle Bart is picking me up but thanks for the offer, Mav."

He looked disappointed but grinned anyway.

"Well then, see you later, O.K?" He asked.

"Yes definitely!" I answered. Before I could talk myself out of it I boldly wrapped my arms around him to give him a quick hug.

He tightly hugged me back, lifting my feet up off the ground before gently putting me back down. We said our goodbyes then Mallory and I went back to work. It was time for the manatees to have their lunch, they are herbivores so mostly kale, romaine lettuce, cabbage, and their very favorite, Broccoli! Hard to believe this is my new normal, but it is.

41: Key deer & the Key to her heart

"I can't believe we are about to graduate and the Wildlife Ranger Academy ends next week! Mallory stated.

"I know, right? I've loved every minute of it and learned so much." I replied.

Mallory and I were currently inside the Key Deer habitat raking up deer poop. Once again not exactly glamorous but I couldn't care less, I would gladly rake up poop to spend time caring for them. Key Deer are absolutely adorable and so sweet. The Key Deer at the park are all been permanently injured, mostly by collisions with automobiles. Not many wildlife organizations were allowed to have Key Deer they are so endangered, but the Homosassa Wildlife park worked very closely with the Florida Wildlife Commission (FWC) and holds special permits to house permanently injured Key Deer while also helping rehabilitate the ones that might eventually be released back to their Florida Keys Big Pine habitat. I sat down on a fallen tree trunk for a moment of rest, and one of the deer I recognized came hobbling over to me. He licked my arm.

"Oh Pogo you are just so freaking cute!" I cooed to him. Pogo is really small and only has 3 legs, but can still out run his keepers.

"Here Rayne, let's give them their treats for the day." Mallory handed me a large bowl of purple grapes while sitting down next to me. Before you could count to 3 we were surrounded by all 6 Key Deer in the habitat. Key Deer love grapes, watching them squash them in their mouths and chew them was priceless. I'd swear you could see them smiling, albeit in a deer kind of way.

"Do you have any plans for tomorrow, Rayne? Why don't we invite Drew and Mav to go out paddle boarding with us? We could tell them we want to look around for C.C. the injured manatee-which of course we will- and see if they want to help." She said with a wink. I laughed at her not-so-subtle explanation.

"And spending time with Drew will just be a bonus, right?"

"Uh, yeah---Captain Obvious!" She laughed too. "Besides, Maverick mentioned he wanted to go looking for him this weekend so it's perfect. As for Drew- I really like him. I can't stop thinking about him! He possibly holds the key to my heart, Rayne. He's so dreamy, smart too. When he says in his South African accent 'Hello Love how are you' I melt faster than chocolate left out in Florida's hot sun. So what do you say, are you in, or are you out?"

"In. All the way. You plan it, I'll be there." I didn't tell her I knew exactly how she felt because I felt the same way about her brother, who possibly held the key to *my* heart! Also, I hadn't gone out on the water all week and this was the perfect opportunity to go out safely surrounded by friends I could trust. I'd have to ask my aunt and uncle for permission, but I know that they completely trust Maverick and would probably be fine with a short excursion on the water with my friends.

"Deal!" Mallory put her hand palm side up and high fived me. "I'll text you later with the deets. This week couldn't have been better, I learned about Manatees and Key Deer with one of my BFF's forever!"

"I *so* agree Mallory. Life *is* good. So Let's go get this weekend started." I gave Pogo one final rub on his neck, saying goodbye to his cute little self. **#KeyDeerCuteness**

Florida Key Deer

Scientific Classification

Kingdom: Animalia

Phylum: Chordata

Class: Mammalia

Order: Artiodactyla

Family: Cervidae

Genus: Odocoileus

The Key Deer (Odocoileus virginianus clavium) is an endangered deer that lives only in the Florida Keys. It is a subspecies of the white-tailed deer (O. Virginianus). It is the smallest North American deer.

Description

This deer can be recognized by its characteristic size, smaller than all other white-tailed deer. Adult males (known as bucks) usually weigh 25-34 kg (55-75 lb) and stand about 76 cm (30 in) tall at the shoulder. Adult females (does) usually weigh between 20 and 29 kg (44 and 64 lb) and have an average height of 66 cm (26 in) at the shoulders. The deer is a reddish-brown to grey-brown in color. Antlers are grown by males and shed between February and March and regrown by June. When the antlers are growing, they have a white velvet coating. The species otherwise generally resembles other white-tailed deer in appearance.

Behavior

Key Deer swim easily between islands.

Living close to humans, the Key deer has little of the natural fear of man shown by most of their larger mainland relatives. The deer are often found in residents' yards and along roadsides where tasty plants and flowers grow. This often results in car-to-deer collisions, as the deer are more active (and harder to avoid) at night. It is not unusual to see them at dusk and dawn, especially on lightly inhabited No Name Key, and in the less-populated northern areas of Big Pine Key.

Breeding occurs all year, but peaks in October and December. Territorial activity is limited to defending a receptive doe from other bucs. Longevity records are 9 years for males and 7 years for females. Adult females form loose matriarchal groups with one or two generations of offspring, while bucs feed and bed together only during the nonbreeding season.

Range, habitat, and diet

The range of the Key Deer originally encompassed all of the lower Florida Keys (where standing water pools exist) but it is now limited to a stretch of the Florida Keys from about Sugarloaf Key to Bahia Honda Key. Key deer use all islands during the wet season when drinking water is more generally available, retreating to islands with a perennial supply fresh water in the dry months.

Key Deer inhabit nearly all habitats within their range, including pine rock lands, hardwood hammocks, mangroves, and freshwater wetlands. The species feed on over 150 plants, but mangroves (red, white, and black) and thatch palm berries make up the most important part of their diets. Pine rockland habitat is important, as well, because it is often the only reliable source of fresh drinking water (Key deer can tolerate drinking only mildly brackish water). Habitat destruction due to human encroachment cause may deer to feed on non-native ornamental plants.

Endangered status

Key Deer were hunted as a food supply by native tribes, passing sailors, and early settlers. Hunting them was banned in 1939, but widespread poaching and habitat destruction caused the sub-species to plummet to near extinction by the 1950's. The National Key Deer Refuge, a federally administered National Wildlife Refuge operated by the Wildlife Service, was established in 1967.

Recent population estimates put the population between 700-800, putting it on the list of endangered species. Road kills from drivers on US 1, which traverses the deer's small range, are also a major threat, averaging between 30 and 40 kills per year, 70% of the annual mortality.

However, the population has made an encouraging rise since 1955, when population estimates ranged as low as 25, and appears to have stabilized in recent years. Still, recent human encroachment into the fragile habitat and the deer's relatively low rate of reproduction point to an uncertain future for species.

42: Searching for C.C. The Manatee

I woke up Saturday morning to the sun shining brightly through my third floor window. I was pretty excited about the paddle board excursion Mallory had orchestrated for us this afternoon so cleverly. She texted me with the time and we were meeting at the Garden of Springs at noon. I smelled the wonderful aroma of food being cooked wafting up to my room so I followed that smell down to the kitchen where my Aunt Beth was busy cooking breakfast.

"Good Morning, Rayne! You look radiant and well rested. I sure hope your hungry because I have made Eggs Benedict and honey butter biscuits." My aunt came over and kissed me on my forehead. I thought that gesture was sweet and I loved her for it.

"I'm famished, Aunt Beth, and it all smells wonderful. Thank you."

"Have some orange juice while you wait. You need to get your strength going because paddle boarding is very strenuous and burns a ton of calories. Today is going to be a scorcher."

"Is it? I have to get used to the hot weather here. I will wear a hat and drink tons of water."

I pretty much inhaled her delicious breakfast. My aunt gave me another waterproof case holder for my phone that I could wear around my neck, leaving my hands free for paddling. She told me she wanted me to have it in case we saw C.C. and needed to make a phone call to the rescue team, but I had a feeling she just bought it for me to have in case of other emergency situations, like the unpleasant kind I encountered at the Manatee Festival. Whatever the reason I took it and thanked her graciously. Her caring for my safety made me feel very loved once again, and sometimes it felt like my mother was still here through her. I realized for the first time that my Aunt Beth probably missed her sister as much as I did only she stayed strong for me. My heart swelled at that thought so I added a huge hug to the thanks holding her tightly for a few moments. When I let her go I noticed she had tears in her eyes, but she was smiling.

"My sister gave me the biggest gift of my life, Rayne, she trusted me with you, her most precious love. I take that very seriously and I'm forever grateful. So please be careful, but have fun. Go be with friends and love life. You deserve it!"

"I will Aunt Beth, it's such a beautiful day to be out on the water."

My mom wanted me happy, and I realized now that I actually was. It still felt like a kick to the stomach whenever I thought of my mom and realized she was no longer here on earth with me. When I lost her I lost a part of my soul, but the rest of my soul was once again filled with joy for life, and filled with love for this family here before me. I insisted on doing the breakfast clean up and when I was finished I went upstairs to change. My uncle offered earlier to drive me down to meet my friends in the golf cart when I was ready, but when I went outside to look for him I got a great surprise. It wasn't my uncle in the drivers seat. It was Maverick, and he was grinning from ear to ear.

"Your chariot awaits, my queen." He gestured to the seat next to him.

"Why thank you me lord!" I giggled, taking that seat next to him. "Where's my Uncle Bart?" I asked.

"He walked down to the dock with Aiden. I walked here to escort you to the Garden of Springs and he suggested we take the golf cart instead and handed me the keys. Mallory and Drew are at the Wildlife Building we can pick them up on the way. My mom called the concessionaire first thing this morning and reserved 4 paddle boards to be taken out at noon, telling them it was for search and rescue efforts concerning CC. They usually rent out all the kayaks and paddle boards on the weekend so that was a good call."

"Yes definitely I didn't think about that. I'd like to own my own paddle board one day. I know they are expensive but I'd use it all the time. Same with a kayak. It's so wonderful to have access to borrowing them, and my aunt and uncle own two kayaks as you already know. I use my Aunt Beth's all the time, I love it. I feel so free when I'm gliding on the water. It's my way of being spiritual. Does that make any sense?" I asked Maverick.

"More than you know, Rayne. When I'm on the water surrounded by nature its very meditative for me. I do all my heavy thinking there." Maverick concurred, gazing at me with his eyes the color of the sea.

I looked back at him feeling a connection as solid as two powerful magnets meeting for the first time.

"Same here Maverick. That's how it is for me." I touched his arm and I felt the most wonderful wave of electricity run throughout my body. I looked down and noticed goosebumps; only this time they weren't mine, they were his.

"We're here." Maverick growled huskily. "Now I have to share you."

"Maybe we can spend some time together later on." I blurted out before I could stop myself.

"There we go thinking the same thing again. Not maybe, but definitely. If I remember correctly, I'm still owed a kiss."

We pulled up to the Wildlife Building, picked up Mallory and Drew, and went on to enjoy a very pleasant afternoon. The only bummer was we didn't see CC anywhere. We saw many other manatees, but not him. Also, Maverick got a phone call that put him in a quiet mood, and we had to end our paddle boarding adventure a little earlier than we wanted so he could go take care of an urgent matter.

Little did I know then that the wonderful afternoon I shared with friends would turn into one of the scariest-yet profound-days of my life.

43: The Rescue

I went home, took a shower, and relaxed a little, but I found I couldn't stop thinking about Serafina and the questions I wanted to ask her. I asked my Uncle Bart if I could drive the golf cart up to the Wildlife Building to do some work concerning my records about Yuma, but I really intended to knock on Serafina's door and have a talk with her about that day I had the unfortunate and unforgettable encounter with the venomous Coral snake. She was there that day, I saw her leave the building in a hurry. I think she lied about being sick, and I wanted to find out why. My instincts were telling me something was up with that, I just couldn't ignore it any longer. After promising to go straight there I quickly reached the Wildlife Building for the second time that day. I went to the back of the building where the Intern rooms were located and was about to knock on Serafina's door when I noticed the door was open just a little. I could hear familiar voices talking from within. To my utter dismay one of those voices belonged to Maverick, the other Serafina's. Before I could stop myself I peeked through the crack of the door. Big mistake, I did not like what I saw at all. Serafina was practically sitting on Mavericks lap, and he was holding her in his arms.

"Maverick, mi querida, you are so good, so brave, so strong! Other guys pale in comparison. What would I do without you?" She said, leaning in to kiss him. I closed my eyes and backed up quietly. I couldn't watch anymore-if I didn't leave and get out of their fast I felt like I would throw up the snack I just ate and they would discover me there intruding, and that would be *mortifying*. As soon as I got out of the Wildlife Building I ran to the golf cart that I could barely see because tears had started to blind me. Stop it! I yelled inwardly at myself. The wind from the golf cart ride helped me dry my tears before I got home. I didn't want anyone to see my misery so I asked Aiden to tell Beth and Bart I was going down to the dock, my sanctuary. I ran all the way there and when I reached the dock I could barely breathe I was so winded, not only from the physical excursion but also from the dam of tears lodged in my throat. I sat on the bench by the water, letting it all go on the river I'd come to love so much. The river that gave me solace, helping to heal me. When I finished and could cry no more, I sat there collecting myself, trying to figure out what it was I just witnessed. How could I have been so wrong about Maverick? What did I miss? Was it possible for him to like me and Serafina at the same time? I was pondering all this when I heard a huge splash in the water. To my utter surprise I saw a manatee with what appeared to be a large crab trap trailing behind it, and it was tangled within the roots of a tree across the river! The poor manatee was struggling to move. It was C.C., and he needed help right now.

"Hold on C.C.!" I said loudly. I grabbed my cell phone out of my pocket to quickly call Ms. Greene to let her know what was happening. She told me to keep an eye on him while she assembled the rescue team to get over there as soon as possible. I hung up and continued to watch him. I realized he had somehow managed to dislodge the crab trap from the tree and was moving slowly away back toward the mouth of the river. Without hesitation I jumped into my aunts kayak, wrapped the life vest around me, and put my phone around my neck with the new case so my hands would be free to paddle after him. I always wore the whistle that Maverick gave me, I would use it to help the rescue team find us. Surprisingly C.C. was able to move pretty steadily considering he had a crab trap wrapped around his tail, because I could clearly see it was his tail and not one of the front flippers as we had originally heard it was. Poor C.C. I thought, that has to be such a burden! After following him for about fifteen minutes he stopped to rest and so did I. That's when I heard the motor of a boat coming closer from behind me. I was relieved to know the rescue team had gotten here so quickly! I turned to face them, waving my arms up in the air to greet them. What I saw instead made my blood turn cold, causing me to drop my arms immediately. It was a grey boat with orange stripes, I knew that boat and who it belonged to. Worse than that-it was moving straight for me- with no intention of stopping. I knew instantly that if I didn't jump out of that kayak right then I'd be seriously hurt if not worse. As I plunged into the water I heard but didn't see the loud whack of the Hicks boat hitting my kayak. I came to the surface of the water relieved for the moment that I was still alive when the first wave hit me, knocking me back under the water. I came up a second time to catch my breath and then another wave tossed the kayak violently forward, causing it to strike the side of my head. It felt as if I got hit with a baseball bat it hurt so bad! For some odd reason I was unable to open my eyes, but could still hear. As I slowly faded into oblivion I heard (why couldn't I open my eyes!) the boat slowly approaching where I was. I also heard two male voices talking to each other.

"Do you think she's still alive?" One voice anxiously asked. "You said you were only going to scare her, not hurt her!"

"Shut yo mouth and grab that phone from her around her neck. Git it!" The other voice snapped back. "We need to see if she has any pictures of us stealing them boat parts."

I felt some tugging around my neck. I knew he had taken my phone.

"I got it!" The first voice declared.

"She'll be alright, she's got a vest on and someone will find her. We got to git away right now, Rod. Go!" He yelled. The boat zoomed away, causing me to rock several more times up and down from the waves of the boats wake. I struggled to stay awake, but I wanted so badly to succumb to the darkness that was threatening to take over my body. Just as I was slipping into unconsciousness something incredible happened. I felt my body being pushed gently through the water. I was able to pry my eyes open just enough to see what was going on. How wonderful, I thought...and then my world faded to black.

44: The Visit

The blackness was only temporary, I could see in the distance the most brilliant and comforting white light enticing me forward. I knew I had left my physical body, a fact proven to me as I could see what was happening to me on the river. My body was draped over Rosie the manatee's body and she was nudging me toward land. I could tell it was Rosie by her rose shaped scar pattern, plus Rosetta her calf was following behind us. How interesting this universe is I mused, I once helped Rosie and now she was helping me! It was cosmic destiny. Everything happens for a reason, as it should. Again the cozy white light enveloped me, I ran toward it. I heard my name called, and even though I never heard that voice before I knew without a shadow of a doubt that it was the voice of my Father beckoning me to come nearer.

"Rayne, our most precious love, we are here." Incredibly, I saw both my parents before me. The pure, exhilarating joy I felt emanated from my every pore.

"Mom! Dad!" I ran to them. They were visions, yes, but they were real too. We weren't touching physically, yet we were connected nonetheless.

"Rayne, it's not your time for this place yet, you have to go back." My father lovingly said to me. He was so handsome and true, I loved him so.

I looked to my Mother. Her warm loving smile instantaneously eased my worries.

"He speaks the truth Rayne, your journey of life has just begun. You have many destinies to fulfill, many adventures yet to live."

"No Mom, I'm staying here with you. I can't lose you again, I won't!" I told her. I was staying here with them and that was final.

"My love you can, and you will." She put her light as a feather hand to my head. What followed was profoundly extraordinary. Remarkably, She showed me visions of some of the wildlife that I would help in the future. When it ended I knew that she was right, I HAD to go back. Not for myself, but for them. I had work to do that was very important.

"You see now, Rayne, don't you? You are going to rescue and save so many of God's creatures, your destiny is to be a Warrior for Wildlife and the Environment. Your actions on Earth will change the wildlife world for the better, and remember this~even the littlest things you do can make a huge difference. Everyone has a destiny. My destiny, Rayne, was to birth and raise you. Your destiny is to help save the environment and the wildlife living in it. We will all be back together one day far into the future, I promise you. You won't remember details about this visit when you go back, but you will know deep down in your soul that we are watching over you, always. Go back now Rayne, fulfill your destiny."

"Go get 'em Tiger!" My dad said, holding my mom in his arms. The perfect ending to a perfect visit. The love aura emanating between our souls was every color of the rainbow and would forever connect us, this I knew. I didn't have to say I loved them, they already knew. I didn't have to say goodbye, because I'd see them again. I turned away from the bright light, looking for my body on Earth. I saw myself half in, half out of the water, covered by some thick underbrush on the bank of the river. I had to do something quick, nobody would be able to see me underneath all that! I ran to the darkness feeling the strong pull of my soul to my body. It connected, at last my eyes could open, but I could not move. I was stuck in

muck and mud, I felt very weak. I was also experiencing a raging headache. I cried like a baby for the second time that day, but this time I shed tears of joy. I was alive, I had seen my parents in Heaven, and I had a very important destiny to fulfill. The details were fuzzy at the moment, though. As I lay there trying to remember I heard more voices in the distance. I recognized one of them. It was Mavericks, and he was calling my name.

"Rayne! Rayne! Can you hear me?" He was yelling way too loudly for my headache.

"I'm here!" I croaked. Why couldn't I talk louder?

"Where could she be, Maverick?" I heard the panicked voice belonging to his twin, Mallory. "Her kayak was upside down in the water, banged up horribly!" She miserably cried.

"I'm over here guys! I'm ok! I said in my mind, because for some very odd reason I was way too tired to speak. Everything seemed to be happening in slow motion. This sucks! I thought glumly. I heard others calling my name from the rescue boat, my Uncle Bart, Sheri the ranger, and Ms. Greene were all looking for me. How would I ever get their attention? Suddenly a lightbulb went on inside my head; My whistle! I could use my whistle that Maverick gave me to call them to me! With my last bit of strength I clumsily grabbed my whistle putting it to my lips. My first blow into the whistle was pathetic. I had to do better than that or they would pass on by me and never even know it. I took a deep breath and tried again, this time it was much stronger. Yes! Yes! I could do this! I did it again and this time it worked, I heard Maverick ask everybody to be quiet because he heard something.

He heard me! I blew it once more. Maverick dove into the river to come to me, I knew that even though I couldn't see it. He reached me quickly. **#MyHero**

"She's over here! I found her!" Maverick yelled to the others.

"Um Mav, could you keep it down, I kind of have a headache." I whispered, possibly croaked.

"Thank God I found you and for the whistle I gave you. Are you hurt? What happened, Rayne?"

What I did next surprised me, Maverick too. I kissed him. I grabbed him by the back of his neck pulling his mouth to mine, kissing him solid for what seemed like a long time but was probably only a few seconds. I kissed Maverick like I meant it, and I did. The kiss felt so good it nullified my headache, but only temporarily. When I finished kissing him I promptly passed out once again.

I didn't fully wake up again until I was in a hospital bed surrounded by those who love me. The first thing I asked them was if they had rescued C.C., and they had, so that was great. My Uncle Bart said he would be just fine now that he was free from the crab trap that had encircled his tail. After treating his injuries and giving him antibiotics he should be able to go back out to the water one day soon. The second thing I asked was if I could go home. Everyone laughed. Maybe it was the pain medication they gave me kicking in, but I felt great. I no longer had a raging headache, it was now just a very mild and manageable roar, and I wanted to be home. Unfortunately the Doctor said I had to stay overnight for "observation." I was a very lucky young lady, he said. I needed to tell my family what had happened to me now and I knew they were not going to like what I had to say. My Uncle Bart told me that Sheriff Lawsy was here to ask me some questions about my accident on the river, which was perfect because I needed to talk to him too. He called him in, and for the next half hour I told them every detail I could about what happened. (Except for the Heaven part, that part I kept to myself, to be forever treasured.) When I was done, I could see the visible anger on my Uncle Bart's face and it was pointed at the sheriff, who looked mad too.

"Don't worry, Bart." Sheriff Lawsy said. "I've got this."

"I believe you, Sheriff. But if any of the Hicks family comes near my niece again they will regret it." Uncle Bart replied.

"That's not all, I have more information." Maverick said from the back of the room, as he walked forward. "We have one more person to talk with, and she's waiting outside the room to talk to us. I'll go get her now."

What happened next was a complete shocker, at least to me. Maverick brought in the last person I ever expected to see, Serafina Serrano. Another shocker? Her beautiful face looked so sad, and she had a bruised and swollen fat bottom lip. Someone hurt her, and we were about to find out exactly who it was.

45: Serafina's Story

"Sheriff Lawsy, this is Serafina Serrano, she's an intern at the Wildlife Park." Maverick introduced her. "I got a phone call from her earlier today asking me to come meet her to talk about something very important. She was hysterically crying and she told me she was scared, not only for her well being but for Rayne's as well. She made me promise to secrecy until we could talk, I agreed to meet her. Now it's time for her to tell you what she told me. Serafina?" Maverick gestured for her take the floor.

Serafina took a deep breath, straightened her posture, and set her sad dark eyes upon me. "lo siento, Rayne, please forgive me. I'm so sorry." She said, with tears falling down her cheeks. My Aunt Beth handed her some tissues to wipe her eyes and she continued. "A couple of weeks ago I met a guy who pursued me relentlessly, kept asking to spend time with me. I thought he was cute, charming, and sweet so I agreed. For a short time it was very nice, I enjoyed his company. I was feeling so insecure about myself, because I had flirted with both Maverick and Drew yet they only wanted to be friends with me." Serafina actually pouted when she said that, as much as she could that is with a fat lip.

"Anyway, he made me feel good about myself, I was flattered. One day he asked me about you, Rayne, just a general question about you coming to live here with your aunt and uncle. I didn't think anything of it, because when I asked him why he cared he said it's a small town and he was just wondering. It was no big deal, he said. So I told him. I was so jealous of you, Rayne, everyone loves you and I could tell Maverick really liked you too. I thought this new guy I met cared about me but I was wrong, very, very, wrong. I am so ashamed of myself!" Serafina broke down crying. My Aunt Beth consoled her, telling her she was doing good and that she was proud of her. A few more minutes later Serafina regained her composure. She continued.

"I told him I was training with you in the reptile department and that's when he must have gotten the idea to do what he did---I *swear* I had no idea he would do anything like he did!" She worriedly looked at my Uncle Bart and the Sheriff, then she looked at me once again.

"He and his brother picked the lock then let the coral snake out, Rayne! He wanted you to get scared or even better yet, hurt. That day I was sick so I called in, remember?"

I nodded yes.

"That afternoon he called me to ask me to meet him at the Reptile House, he said he was visiting the park with a friend. He begged me to give him a private tour, so despite not feeling good I agreed to meet with him. I found out this morning that his friend was his older brother and that he used him to distract me while he rigged the back door to stay open after we left. That's how he got in, it was him that let the snake out of its habitat! He used me to get to you Rayne. I had no idea, I hope you believe me. When I found out later what had happened to you and Drew in the Reptile House I wondered how that could have happened, but I never suspected it was because of the guy I was dating."

"Serafina, are you saying that the guy you are talking about admitted to you that he tried to kill Rayne?" The sheriff incredulously inquired.

"He said that he was only trying to scare her, because she meddled in his family's business." Serafina told him.

"Continue. Please." The Sheriff said.

"I heard about what happened to you that day at the Manatee Festival Rayne, and I became suspicious that it was him who pushed you down and threatened you. Maverick told me the day after it happened because he saw me talking to him at the festival. What Maverick didn't know was that I was on a date with him that day. Maverick asked me why I was talking to him, I lied and said he just asked me a question, I didn't know him. Maverick said that was good because he was really bad news. After that I started to put the puzzle pieces together, because I was the reason he knew you were going to be at the festival...I told him! Half way through our date at the festival he said he had to go to the restroom, disappearing for a long time. I think that's when he went to you and threatened you." She paused and took a sip of water from a glass that my Aunt Beth had brought to her. She winced when the glass hit her bottom lip.

"How did you get that injury to your lip, Serafina?" The Sheriff asked.

Serafina's eyes swelled up with tears again, then spilled down her face. "From him, Sheriff. He hit me!"

I felt so bad for her, it was obvious she was heartbroken and my heart hurt for hers.

"Can you finish your story, Serafina? You're almost done. You've done great so far." Maverick assured her.

"Sí....yes. I have to. I kept my distance from him after I heard that from Maverick, that is, until a couple of days ago after we all had lunch together, and I heard that Rayne went to the police station to fill out an incident report about her assault and threat. I left the table as soon as I heard that, I had to talk to him because I was hoping he would reassure me that he had nothing to do with it! I called him and he said he wanted to talk to me in person, that he didn't do anything wrong. I wanted to believe him so I agreed to meet with him. That was a big mistake." She shook her head in dismay.

"He came to the park and we went for a walk on the tram trail. I told him what I heard, as I did he became very agitated. I finally realized that he was *not* the nice guy he professed to be. *El no es bueno!!!* I asked him again if he was the one who threatened Rayne, and this time he confessed it to be true. He said that you were threatening his family business, you had taken pictures of his brothers up to no good and had to be dealt with accordingly. I told him I wanted no part of his craziness and that I was going to have to tell Rayne's Uncle Bart what I knew. I will never forget the rage in his eyes when I said that-he looked so hateful and angry! How could I ever have thought he was handsome? That he was nice? Soy estùpido!"

"You are *not* stupid, Serafina. Please don't say that. We all make mistakes." I told her.

"But I am Rayne! As soon as I said that to him I tried to walk away from him but he grabbed my arm, swung me around, and slapped my face so hard! He told me if I said one word to anybody about any of this I would very much regret it! He didn't say he would hurt me more but I understood what he meant. Fortunately for me we heard a tram coming closer, that jarred him out of the rage he was feeling toward me and he quickly left. The last thing he said to me was, "you walked into a door, understand? We wouldn't want pretty Serafina's face to get more injuries, now would we?" I walked home quickly and called Maverick. I didn't know what else to do, he knew this guy, he had warned me about him previously." She finished her story.

Maverick looked at Sheriff Lawsy. "The guy she's talking about sheriff? His name is Rod. Rodney Hicks, to be exact."

"Yes that's him!" I told the room. "I heard his name mentioned when I was in the water. They deliberately tried to hit my kayak with their boat! They also took my phone when I was slipping into unconsciousness."

"As you already know Rayne we have been investigating the Hicks family for months now, we suspected they were operating a chop shop at their old Homosassa homestead, stealing expensive boats and boat parts and equipment then selling them. Your pictures were just what we needed to get an official search warrant. The Hicks homestead is being searched right now as we speak, the Hick Brothers arrested. You girls don't have to worry anymore about coming across the Hicks family ever again, because they are going to be in jail for a very long time. I will still need you Serafina to come to the station and make an official statement."

"I will Sheriff." She promised.

"Bart can I talk to you privately in the waiting room?" He asked my uncle.

"Yes of course, Sheriff. Maverick why don't you take Serafina home now, Beth is going to stay the night here at the hospital and Rayne needs some rest. She's had quite a day." He smiled at me. "Get some rest, honey, hopefully you can come home tomorrow."

"Yes sir, I will." Maverick told my uncle, walking over to me. "Goodnight for now, I'll see you tomorrow." He came up to me and kissed me on the forehead.

Serafina came up to me next, and she grabbed my hands.

"I am truly sorry, Rayne. Will you ever forgive me?" She asked.

"Serafina there is nothing to forgive. We both stumbled upon the same bad guy, that's all. Let's put all this past us and move forward. I'd like to be friends."

I thought I was through being shocked but then something else shocking happened. Serafina Serrano hugged me hard, and told me she'd like that more than anything else in the world. Everyone left, with Beth promising to come back soon. I finally did rest, I was exhausted. Today had been an astonishing day and I was glad to see it end.

46: A Gift before Graduation

I spent the next day recuperating and taking it easy, never leaving my couch and cozy abode. All of my new friends came by to check on me (including Serafina) to see if I was alright after all the crazy drama I had experienced at the hands of the Hicks Brothers. Their arrests and the subsequent discovery of their chop shop in old Homosassa made the front page of the Citrus County Chronicle, news travels fast in Citrus County. Thankfully there were no mentions of me, the Sheriff promised my Uncle Bart that it wouldn't be necessary to divulge that information. Interestingly enough, Rod Hicks confessed to everything. Perhaps deep down he had a conscience, one could hope. My Aunt Beth felt sorry for him to some degree because he grew up in a toxic environment, a very unhealthy, unsavory, and criminal environment. I prayed that he would get help for his anger and one day maybe lead a proper life.

"Do you realize you essentially saved the lives of 2 manatee Rayne?" Mallory asked me when she came to visit me with Maverick.

"Oh no, I can't take that credit, I just did what any of us would do. The real heroes are the Wildlife staff caring for C.C. at the Manatee Hospital.

"C.C. is doing great, by the way, I checked on him before I came here." Maverick added. "Give yourself some credit Rayne, I saw you that day with Rosie, it's like she heard you, as crazy as that sounds."

If he thought that sounded crazy I could just imagine what he'd think if I told him that I think Rosie helped save my life after the kayak hit my head and knocked me unconscious. I'll keep that little fact to myself for the time being, I decided. I was still trying to process that profound experience. I was very glad to hear about C.C. though. I would never regret following him even if it meant my personal life might be in danger. Here's the thing-I knew I shouldn't have gone after C.C. by myself, but I did. I couldn't stop myself, and I didn't want to. I will spend the rest of my life doing anything and everything I can to help wildlife in need. It's that simple. After my friends left my Aunt Beth came up to my room to give me the most wonderful gift, a beautiful dress for me to wear to the Wildlife Ball Saturday night.

"I went shopping for you while your friends were here visiting you, Rayne. Consider it an early graduation gift~you've excelled at Wildlife Ranger Academy, Bart and I are so proud of you! I think this dress will look lovely on you. It's the same color as your eyes. I just know your mom would want me to do this for you, I miss her so much!" Beth's blue eyes were shiny with unshed tears.

"I miss her too, Aunt Beth! Thank you so much for thinking of me!" I ran to her and hugged her tight, my own eyes blurring with tears of both sadness *and* happiness.

"Will you try it on for me?" She asked, unzipping the garment bag, revealing a dress so pretty I gasped out loud. The dress was made of emerald green silk with a sheer green chiffon overlay. The top part was halter style, high on the neck. The bottom was a fully pleated skirt, the kind that you just know was going to swirl around your knees as you moved. Beth also bought me a thin gold belt to wrap around my waist.

"It's gorgeous Aunt Beth, I'm so touched you did this for me. I can't wait to try it on, of course I will!" I excitedly ran to the bathroom to try it on. The dress did not disappoint. It was the first grown up dress I had ever worn, and when I walked out to show Beth she was the one that gasped out loud.

"It's perfection, Rayne. You're stunning. Wow."

I walked to the full length mirror to see myself in the dress. Not only did it fit perfectly, it made me feel like a million bucks. The chiffon and silk fabrics felt so luxurious on my body. I was grateful for the natural golden tan that I had acquired from practically living on the water in my spare time.

"I love it, Aunt Beth. And I love you."

"I Love you more!" She declared. "Now all we need is a pair of shoes to go with it and I'd love to style your hair for the party. Maybe we can put it up somehow to show off the neckline. What do think?"

I told my Aunt I'd like that then she left to make me something to eat after I promised her to put my pajamas back on and get some more rest. I did so willingly after hanging my dress up where I could see it and stare at it until I got to wear it again. I was tired but content and ready for my last week of Wildlife Ranger Academy. It's been quite the fun adventure, I was pretty sad to see it end but grateful for the chance to have experienced it. I didn't know what was next but I was about to find out that my life was going to take another unexpected turn, one I never saw coming.

47: One Adventure ends, another begins

Our last week of Wildlife Ranger Academy was a whirlwind of activity. We went back to the previous animal departments we had trained at, only this time without supervision. We had to make diets by ourselves, clean the habitats, and record notes and observations. I loved every single moment of it. Ms. Greene and my Aunt Beth also required us to create and design our "Wildlife" resumes. We had to include the duties and responsibilities we accomplished, public relations and events we experienced, and log the amount of hours we spent working with the different wildlife at the park. They wanted our resumes to reflect the working knowledge we had gained while attending the Jr. Wildlife Ranger Academy. I downloaded a resume app on my iPad and had fun customizing it, I even included a picture of a manatee on the top right corner, which I felt was a nice touch to stand out. We graduated Friday afternoon and were given official Florida Park Service Certifications of Wildlife Management, as well as letters of recommendations from the Wildlife Park Manager, (my Uncle Bart) and from Mallory and Maverick's mom Ms. Greene, the Wildlife Park Supervisor and park Veterinarian. We were all set to begin our future careers. All of the park employees and volunteers came to our graduation ceremony held at the park's Garden of Springs overlooking the Homosassa

River. They clapped for us, cheering us on as we accepted our new Wildlife Certifications. It was a day of love, encouragement, and acceptance. After the graduation ceremony we were treated to a delicious lunch of grilled veggie dogs, pasta with ranch dressing, and fruit salad at the picnic pavilion. The Wildlife Ball would be a celebration party tomorrow night, it was something we were all looking forward to. It would be the perfect ending to a wonderful adventure, for sure. Mallory and Jenzy were coming over to my house to get ready with me before the Ball and I was beyond excited. I was cleaning my room for the get together with the girls tomorrow before the Wildlife Ball when I was called down to the living room for a family meeting. I found out that another good thing in my life was about to end, and it was an interesting surprise I never saw coming.

"Please take a seat and get comfortable Rayne, we need to have a serious talk as a family." My Uncle Bart said to me. I sat down on the couch next to Aiden.

"What about, Uncle Bart?" I asked.

"Let me start by stating the obvious, we are a family, and we make decisions together. But sometimes an opportunity comes your way in your professional career, one that cannot be rejected nor denied. Beth and I have had to make a life decision, now it's time to share the news with you and Aiden. We hope you will be as excited as we are, because it's going to be a new wonderful adventure for all of us." He gazed at my Aunt Beth and smiled. She took over from there.

"Kids, Bart has been asked to become the new Manager at another state park located in South Florida. The Park is called Bill Baggs Cape Florida State Park and is located on an Island called Key Biscayne. Key Biscayne is part of Miami. This is an incredible opportunity, we should all be very proud of him being promoted, as the park is one of the most important parks in the Florida Park Service. I know I am." She gazed back at my uncle with genuine love and appreciation.

"Aiden, what do you think about this?" She asked him.

"I think it's epically awesome!" He excitedly replied.

Her attention now focused on me. "Rayne? What about you? We know you've been through so much, so many changes. You just moved here, and now we are asking you to move once again. Your opinion means so much to us. How do do feel about this?"

I sat quietly for just a moment, letting it all sink in. Then I answered her question. It was an easy answer, because I knew it was a new life adventure, and I was all in. I had only one reply, it was a no brainer.

"I'm with Aiden. When do we move?" I asked, and we all laughed. And just like that, my life was going to change once more.

48: Getting Ready for the Ball

As exciting as that news was it only got better. My uncle explained that one important reason he wanted to accept the job was the fact that he would be able to hand pick his top staff to work with him. The current management at the park were retiring or about to retire, including the State Park's resident Biologist. Hiring Joni Greene was my uncle's first choice as she was both a Biologist and Veterinarian and would be a perfect fit. So that meant the Greene family was moving to the Island as well and would also be living on property. I couldn't have asked for anything more perfect than that. I could not wait to talk to them about this!

"What about Jenzy's family, Uncle Bart?" I had to ask about my dear friend.

"For now her father will stay at this park, but only temporarily. The current Assistant Park Manager at Bill Baggs State Park retires in 6 months and when he does I will ask Jenzy's dad to join us there. That's good isn't it?" My uncle asked me.

"Very." I answered. We continued to talk more about the move until Jenzy and Mallory came over to stay the night and get ready for the party. Mallory was just exploding with excitement about both the party and the news she had just been given to her from her mother about the move.

"Oh my goodness! Is this really happening?" She asked while pulling me in to a hug the moment she saw me. I hugged her back.

"It's definitely happening!" I walked over to Jenzy and gave her a big hug like the one Mallory just gave me. "And you'll be joining us all soon Jenzy! Isn't life great??? I'm moving and both of my best friends are too!"

"It's so exciting and I know time will fly by. You two won't forget me until I get there will you?" Jenzy asked.

"As if that was possible girlfriend!" Mallory declared.

"Never in a million years Jenzy! And your right, 6 months will just fly by." I assured her.

"I've never heard of Key Biscayne, have you guys?" Jenzy looked our way.

"No, I haven't." Mallory answered her. "But when I told Serafina about the news she was very happy for us! She said it's a very exclusive, family oriented Barrier Island famous for its historic Lighthouse just 10 minutes away from Downtown Miami. She also mentioned that she goes with her family on special occasions to the Island to eat at a famous seafood restaurant on the water that overlooks Downtown Miami. She said at night the downtown skyline shines brightly in the distance."

I added that I didn't know anything about Key Biscayne but would be googling it soon to learn whatever I could, after the Wildlife Ball was over.

"I know one thing, Dolls." Mallory said very seriously.

"What's that Mallory?" I curiously asked her.

"It's time to celebrate our lives, our friendships, and our Graduation! Let's put on some music and let the festivities begin! We have a Ball to attend to!" She said with a delightfully dramatic flair.

Jenzy and I laughed with her and we spent the next couple of hours listening to music, dancing, and talking girl talk. We admired each other's outfits; Mallory was wearing a deep burgundy dress that complimented her blonde hair perfectly and Jenzy decided to wear a chic all white tuxedo outfit. She looked very sophisticated I thought. They loved my green dress, Mallory said she thought it looked ethereal, so delicate and airy. Jenzy got out her professional makeup kit and applied our makeup. Her skills are on point and when she was finished both Mallory and I were thrilled. She managed to highlight our features creating a natural but glowing effect that complimented our dresses. In my case she used a light pink blush on my cheeks and dusted my eyes with a shimmering rose gold eyeshadow. She also thinly lined my eye with black eyeliner and coated my eyelashes with jet black mascara. The shimmering eyeshadow reminded me of the shoes I had picked up a few nights prior shopping with my aunt. I knew when I saw them they perfect. They were gladiator style sandals that were a soft metallic gold accented with the same colored medal studs. The straps zippered up to the top of my knees. They were both gorgeous *and* comfortable. **#WinWin** My Aunt fixed my hair into a casual knot on top of my head after curling my hair. She pinned it up with small gold crystal clips and left just a few tendrils of my hair falling down around my face framing it in just the right places. I put on my favorite pair of small gold hoop earrings and finished my look by applying a slightly glossy, lightly pink tinted lip gloss on my lips.

"You look like a celestial goddess Rayne! Hold on I have something in my make up kit for us as a surprise." Jenzy said as she rummaged through her kit.

"Here they are!" She showed us what she was holding.

"Are those the metallic temporary tattoos that I have seen everyone wearing now?" Mallory asked.

Jenzy nodded her head yes. "I bought them thinking it would be fun for us to wear them tonight. Let's pick out some to wear and I'll apply them." She laid them out on my coffee table.

"*Ooohhhh* they are gorgeous Jenzy!" Mallory claimed. "Thank you!"

There were so many cool designs to choose from, designs that looked like bracelets or necklaces, or just single tattoos that could be applied.

My favorite were the animal ones, Peacocks, Owls, dolphins, sea turtles, Elephants, among others. That is, until I saw the glittery golden stars and moon tattoos.

"What do you think about these you guys, will they go with my outfit?" I asked.

"*ABSOFREAKINGLUTELY RAYNE!*" Mallory squealed. I laughed. Mallory is so larger than life-she makes every time a good time.

"She's right, Rayne. And I know just where to put them." Jenzy got to work and before I knew it I had a tattoo bracelet made of stars and moons around my left wrist and a crescent moon with two small stars framing my right eye. When I saw myself in the mirror I almost could not believe how I looked. For the first time in my life I actually felt pretty, I hoped Maverick would think the same. The anticipation of seeing him later was almost overwhelming.

"I love them, Jenzy. Thanks you so much." I told her. Mallory and Jenzy picked their designs, Mallory chose Sea Stars and Seahorses and Jenzy chose an intricate geometric design that glimmered on her skin like a necklace. We took tons of selfies and pictures and my Aunt Beth proclaimed we were the most glamorous girls she had ever seen. By the time we finished the sky was turning to dusk, the vibrant deep fuchsia pink Florida sunset was as beautiful as ever. We could feel the excitement and anticipation in the air around us, it was so palpable I felt like I could touch it. We were ready for the Wildlife Ball.

49: The Wildlife Ball

averick came to pick us up in the 8 passenger golf cart belonging to the park. We decided to go together as a group instead as individual dates, Jenzy suggested that since we all have been a team from the very beginning we should stay a team at the end. We all heartily agreed.

"Well check this out!" Mallory drawled. "Florida's version of a limousine!" She laughed and so did everyone else.

"Hello gorgeous gals!" Drew looked at us with appreciation. "My Ladies you are spectacularly beautiful tonight! Maverick, can you believe our good fortune?" He asked.

Maverick was looking only at me.

"*Wow.*" he silently said, but I could read his lips. That one simple silent word sent intoxicating shivers down my spine. **#Score!**

I blushed under his direct gaze, almost pinching myself to see if this was actually happening. How could I be so lucky to have such a handsome young man staring at me with such straight up admiration? Maverick was wearing dark jeans, a crisp white dress shirt, and an expensive looking dark blue blazer that fit him perfectly. He walked over to me ignoring everyone else around us.

"Rayne." He said, taking my hand. "You take my breath away you look so pretty. May I escort you to the Ball?" He asked.

"You may indeed." I replied with a huge smile of my own.

Maverick drove us the Wildlife Ball being held at the Visitor Center at the main entrance of the park. The center was transformed into a Safari themed party complete with white lights strung from the banners highlighting a jungle like atmosphere. There were large poster sized pictures of the animals residing at the park on the walls, and the tables were laden with food in chafing dishes, making the whole room smell wonderfully delicious. There was even a dessert table with a chocolate fountain. By far my favorite thing at the party though was the photo booth, and we all took turns getting our pictures taken with the funny props they had provided to use. I laughed so much my sides started to ache. Maverick asked me to take pictures with just him in the photo booth, I happily obliged. When we finished Maverick took my hand and whisked me away to the outside terrace overlooking the water. The air was cool with a slight breeze and the light of the glowing silvery moon beckoned in the distance. There was nobody out there but us.

I started to tell him how nice it was out on the terrace when Maverick did something so unexpected yet so wonderful~he swirled me around and leaned in to kiss me. When our lips touched it felt magical, so *right*. I swear my knees went weak and I probably would have fallen if it wasn't for one of his strong arms that was wrapped around my waist. His other hand was holding the back of my head. I was immediately consumed with his kisses, the world around me ceased to exist. When we finally pulled apart I opened my eyes slowly, savoring the tingling feeling his kisses left on my lips. I could not help but be delighted when I saw the intensely satisfied smile on his face. I now knew what the big deal was about chemistry, and we had it, big time.

"I've been wanting to do that for so long, Rayne, it's practically all I think about. Are you glad I did?" He asked while still holding me close.

"Glad?" I said with a smile. "Does this answer your question?" I said, pulling him into another kiss, this one lasting a little bit longer.

We kissed for what seemed like an eternity but in reality was just a few minutes. I would have loved to continue making out with Maverick but he took my hand and led me to a nearby bench.

"The first time I met you I was blown away." Maverick professed. "I was mesmerized by your delighted response to meeting Rose the Manatee, capturing my attention as I tied the kayak up to the ladder on the dock. You were so engrossed by your meeting with Rose you never even heard me, which afforded me a few minutes to watch you in silence. When you turned around and I saw your face for the very first time, it was as if time had stopped and I had known you all along, but never met you until now. Does that make sense?" I nodded yes then he continued. "You looked happy and sad at the same time, strong yet vulnerable, hopeful but jaded, everything contradictory and so intriguing. I thought to myself, how can that be? How could I see so many emotions coming from her in just one encounter? I wasn't sure, but I knew instantly right there you were *the one*. He reached into his jacket and pulled out a small rectangular box, opening it to show me the most precious gift, a lovely rose gold heart shaped locket with a matching long delicate chain. It glimmered prettily against the backdrop of the luminous moon.

"Rayne Lanecaster, will you be my girlfriend?"

"Maverick it's exquisite! I love it! And *YES!* Yes I would love to be your girlfriend!" I threw my arms around him pulling him to a hug.

"I thought you could put a picture of your parents in the locket, so they would always be close to your heart. The rose gold reminds me of the color of your hair and also represents your love for Rose the manatee.

I slipped the locket on. It was quite possibly the sweetest, most thoughtful gift he could ever have given me. We talked about the future, taking our budding relationship one day at a time, slow and steady. I felt safe and secure in his arms, so content. I wanted to savor every minute of this spectacular night of my life, memorize everything about this party, and this wonderful place. I do not know how I knew this, but innately I knew that I would never be here ever again. My life was about to take me to a new adventure of the wild kind, and I could not wait to see what came next. **#KeyBiscayneHereICome**!